# *Captured Souls*

*Sèphera Girón*

First e-book published by Samhain Horror Publishing in 2010.

Scarlett Publishing

Copyright 2017 Cover by Scarlett Publishing

Copyright 2017 Katrina Brown cover photo image

Copyright 2017 Sèphera Girón

Praise for *Captured Souls*:

"In *Captured Souls*--her latest erotic thrill ride, Sèphera Girón has created a terrifying new character: a female rendition of Dr. Frankenstein given to detailed scientific human experimentation combined with the sexually predatory and obsessive nature of Nabokov's Humbert Humbert. Horrific and unforgettable." -- Lisa Mannetti, Bram Stoker Award-winning author of *The Gentling Box* and *Deathwatch*

"Sèphera Girón knocks that stereotypical male sexual predator on his head. You won't find another book like this one out there. If you want lust, insanity and horror plaited together into one easy and fun-to-read diabolical story, *Captured Souls* is for you!" --Nancy Kilpatrick, *Revenge of the Vampir King*

"A queasily beguiling blend of erotica and body horror, Sephera Giron's *Captured Souls* pits a sexy female mad scientist with a literal fetish for fleshy modification against the self-set challenge of not just finding the perfect lover, but making one. Think Frankenstein in a bustier, with a cool, sleek, Cronenbergian edge. The result is an imaginative Grand Guignol freakout with porno flair, pumped full of dry black humor and nasty surprises, explicit in every way possible--overall, quite disgustingly entertaining." -- Gemma Files, *Experimental Film*

# Captured Souls

*Sèphera Girón*

# Table of Contents

*Notes and Journals of Dr. Miriam Frederick re: Experiment 698*

*Journal*

In examining the human experience, one realizes that perfection appears in many forms for many people. What is perfection for one may not be perfection for another.

Beauty. Brains. Brawn.

Honesty. Loyalty. Intelligence.

Flawless flesh. Physical symmetry. Sexual stamina.

Quick wit. Compassion. Lust.

What are the qualities that define perfection?

Perspective?

In the end, if there were a type of mate one could have, one could choose, perhaps create, that human being would likely encompass enhanced qualities of intelligence, beauty and physical stamina.

Almost any human has a wish list and I think we all have the same one. How we view the potential candidates on our wish lists is somewhat subjective, although intelligence and stamina are measurable. Physical beauty or handsomeness is a more subjective commodity.

Is it even possible to find one human being with enhanced qualities of intelligence, beauty and stamina?

What lengths would I go through to find such a mate?

Would it ever be possible to create one mate out of three or more? Or would it be more preferable to have a polygamous arrangement to satisfy each facet of desire as it arises?

What would I provide in return? After all, there needs to be an exchange to keep the universal laws of equilibrium in balance.

My undying love and loyalty, a home, financial stability and endless nights of ecstasy would be part of their own personal paradise. I think it could be an equal trade if I find the right specimens.

My journals and observations will record the emotional and physical progress of my latest experiments.

This journal will contain my more subjective observations. There is another book filled with my detailed calculations, charts and formulas. The two books remain separate in case of damage or theft.

So my new quest begins.

*Experiment Number 698*

*Specimen 1*

When I first spied him across the room, I suspected he would indeed be a worthy candidate for experiment number 698. It was indicated by a punch in my solar plexus. The visuals were perfection, no question. Until I met him, exchanged verbiage with him and interacted with him, I couldn't quite be certain if he would be as intelligent as I anticipated. There he stood, long and lanky, in the doorframe that connected the party room to the hallway, his shoulders slightly slouched as he drew on a cigarette, blue eyes staring directly at me.

He watched me, hypnotic, glittering eyes observing my every movement. Calculating. Predatory. The idea of it amused me. His youth was intoxicating. The fact that anyone dared to smoke inside at a party anymore was also an indication that this rebel with a pen could be just what the doctor ordered.

The chattering noises and laughter of our mutual academic friends drinking around us faded from my consciousness as I saw only him.

Lion to prey. Tony to Maria. Dr. Frank-N-Furter to his Rocky. Dr. Miriam Frederick to Author Scott Gravenhurst.

I walked towards the honored guest, prim in my three-piece, grey skirt suit and sky-high stilettos, a predatory slink in my gait. He kept his stance in the doorframe as I stepped past him, lightly brushing his chest with my elbow on the way through to the patio.

Summer air was warm on my face. A light breeze rippled through the mature trees that lined the gardens of the faculty building.

He followed me.

"Dr. Miriam Frederick," I said as I held out my hand to him. He took it and instead of shaking it, he lightly brushed his lips to it.

"Charmed," he said and released my hand. "Scott Gravenhurst."

"Ah, yes. Our visiting guest," I said, pretending to stare around for someone more important. I waved towards a nobody and turned my attention back towards Specimen 1.

"Yes, I'm here for a few days," he said. His gaze traveled from my carefully slicked-back bobbed hair, my full red lips and then down my sleek figure.

When his attention returned to my eyes, he stammered. Very slightly. My green contacts were working their ethereal magic.

"Mmm…Ms. Frederick," he said.

I licked my lips, breathing in the sweetness of the nervous sweat underneath his Jimmy Dean persona.

"Yes, Scott," I smiled, coyly.

"Isn't the moonlight lovely tonight?" he led me out farther onto the patio.

"Toronto is beautiful this time of year," I told him. "We have the most beautiful summers. Can you hear the leaves whisper?"

"Yes, they're telling me that there are many secrets to be shared."

He smoked his cigarette as we both stared at the stars and the moon. The murmurs of people farther in the gardens mingled with the light classical soundtrack that filled the ancient halls of the old faculty building.

He began to recite a poem. I joined in and we laughed together.

After several poems, we stopped and the distant murmuring and tinkling of glasses became backdrop ambiance once more.

"I guess another drink is in order," he said, noting my empty glass.

"Most definitely," I said and slipped my hand through his as we navigated through the clumps of people. I was as tall as he was, my shoes were so high. The view of people giving me darting glances was easier to see elevated above most.

There were a few raised eyebrows aimed in my direction but I didn't mind. My nights with various colleagues left different imprints, even years later. I stopped mingling with my cohorts long ago as it became apparent that some people can't split their alliances to the different compartments of their lives. Complications and emotional drama only waste time that can be better focused on making progress in one's field.

Even wives can't seem to forgive me, even though I never wanted their spineless wonders for more than a few hours. But my importance to the university is incalculable, so the disenchanted put up with my idiosyncrasies. If not for me and most of the people in this room, there wouldn't be grant money for parties, studies, renovations and home laboratories. Behavior Systematic Neurological Studies is in big demand in these times of psychopaths and terrorists. So we all keep our secrets and each other's.

I smiled at my conquests as I let Specimen 1 order me another glass of wine and we found a nook in the room to stare out at the party. University bigwigs gossiped in little cliques, whispering, no doubt mostly about me, likely seeing the innocent act of Specimen 1 bringing me a glass of wine as me luring him into my lair. Which I am, of course, but it's not seemly to be gossiping right in front of my face.

"Your peers?" Specimen 1 asked as he caught me frowning.

"Colleagues, perhaps," I said, drinking deeply from the wine he gave me. "However, most of my friends aren't from the university. And my colleagues rarely see me. I do the majority of my work in my home laboratory. More convenient."

"Oh," he said. "What do you do?"

"I'm a scientist but I love to read, which is why I'm here tonight," I started to walk so that we weren't trapped in a corner. "I love to mingle with authors and publishers. I also love to go dancing. Clubs. Parties. Probably not really the run-of-the-mill geek you conjured up in your mind."

"You're too beautiful to be a scientist," he said. His youthful earnestness slipped out for a moment from the too-cool-for-school author pose.

"You're very kind," I said.

"I've always been intrigued by mature women," he said.

My dear writer boy did not disappoint. He was indeed the classic womanizer.

My heart raced as he spoke; he had a wonderfully crisp accent that I could have listened to for hours. He was only in town for a few days, a special guest-author speaker at the university as part of a seminar series. We easily bantered about books. His face was lean and he had an air of sadness about him. He writes about dark things, maybe because he's lived them or maybe now that he's drawn such ideas in with his fantasies, they haunt his reality. It will be interesting to find out.

I will find out.

The more we drank, the more ideas we seemed to share. I was deliciously warm, lightheaded and fidgeting in hormonal overdrive from Specimen 1's pheromones.

"Tell me about your next book," I asked him. "What is it about?"

"I've just signed a three-book deal with a major publisher to write about a fictional dark world of psychological madness."

"How delightful," I nodded.

"Tell me about your experiments, Doctor," he whispered, tilting my head up with his fingers tucked under my chin. I stared into his eyes as the warmth of his soft lips lightly brushed mine.

"Come with me and I'll show you," I said, taking his hand and leading him out of the party room and down the hallway.

The fluorescent lights buzzed and hummed noisily as my heels clicked along the marble tiles. I passed three doors and stopped at the fourth. I was in luck. The small staff bathroom was open, complete with two comfortable chairs and a table. I pulled him in and locked the door behind us.

I pushed him into one of the leather chairs and straddled him, hiking my tight skirt up as I slid along his long legs.

"My, Doctor." The words passed his lips when I pressed my mouth against his.

What happened next sealed his fate. Specimen 1 was nicely endowed and we kept pace in frenzied secret lust. When the chair lost its intrigued, I lay on the floor, his breath hot on my neck as he impaled me.

As my hands clutched his back beneath his shirt, his flesh warming me inside and out, I thought about the next phase of my experiment and his place in it.

I came once, twice, three times in that little bathroom. His climax was accompanied by a loud cry and then my name whispered into the crook of my neck.

We lay on the floor for a moment, I savored the delightful smoothness of his young, firm skin. His sweat mingled with mine until at last, he pulled himself out and off of me. He was almost coy as he slid his pants back up. I laughed.

"A most excellent party, Doctor," he grinned.

"Welcome to Toronto," I smiled.

We returned to the party and made our rounds. He was whisked away by his hosts to be introduced around the room. I stood alone mostly, dodging glares from spurned suitors.

At one point, I approached the book-club clique of behavioral scientists and tried to shoehorn my way into their conversation. I let them prattle at me, and I them, while I watched as Specimen 1 was led outside and, thus, to the taxi that would send him off to his hotel.

*Journal*

I continue with my work, struggling to perfect my slippery idea into reality. A complicated, yet surprisingly simple, concept.

It was time to build the family.

There needed to be a way to entice someone to want to be part of a team. My team. But would the team players know about each other? *Should* they know about each other?

Loneliness is a fear for most. Sexual compatibility is something we all crave. With sexual compatibility, there would be no loneliness.

Part of my research involves capturing that moment when everything seems so perfect—two bodies, two hearts beating against each other, flesh warm against flesh. Anything else on earth, one can do for one's self. But to have someone's arms around you while they are in you, that needs partnership.

And in that moment of perfection, when everything feels "exactly right", there must be a way to capture that sensation and relive it again and again.

•Rewire the brain to crave specific things—people, objects, fetishes…

•Electrical impulses. A device to transmit that isn't obvious. Something simple like a cell phone or an MP3 player, a GPS, a laptop, a hearing aid

•Create an environment to stimulate and placate the primary obsession or creative impulse

•Create a home where obsessions are appreciated and sexual lifestyles and appetites are compatible.

•Create a family, a relationship. Is one person (for example, one man, one woman) enough for anyone after a year or two?


How can I capture that moment of bliss, of comfort, of exact unity, and keep it forever?


*Journal*

The ideas of perfection haunt me. The perfect man. The perfect love. The perfect relationship. The perfect lifestyle.

Is it possible to delve completely into our art forms and obsessions yet still enjoy perfect sexual bliss with another?

That moment of orgasm, of flesh against flesh, contained and examined and drawn out in real life, real time, had to be freeze-framed and captured.

Is it folly to think that because something was good once, it could be again, even though it's beyond the time when it sank to banality?

Why do wonderful experiences happen once or twice between two people, only never to be re-created?

Even when both parties are willing, fresh chemistry has vanished, never to be replicated as the cells begin to remember and form new habits.

Can I re-create the initial chemistry and keep the baseline constant so that every time is like the first "good" time?

*Journal*

In looking around my lab, my basement, really, of this mammoth, old gothic three-story house with attic I bought a couple of years ago, I study the degrees, awards and clippings I have framed around the room. It takes time to dust them. I don't allow the cleaning service down into my lab; they can dust the upstairs trophies and plaques. The acclaims down here are more specific. The awards for isolating genes and cells. The recognition for my work with serial killers and criminal psychopaths. Awards and articles pairing sexual desire and deviancy towards specific behavioral traits and personalities.

As the psychiatric labels are written and rewritten in endless textbooks, I continue my various researches, more interested in experiments than in labels.

My successes are many and varied, but only the most prestigious are displayed. Some of these victories resulted in accompanying financial bonuses, always an irony in my field of study since large paychecks from various universities and grants gave me more money than I'd ever truly spend. Most of my life consists of earnestly conducting my experiments and making notes such as these; where will I spend hundreds of thousands of dollars? My experiments are expensive but still don't reach the grant amounts. I keep much of the excess cash hidden in various panels throughout the house. Locations will be specified in my will, which will likely be with this diary at my death.

On the main floor, I have a home gym with all the state-of-the-art equipment, though I like to leave the house to go work out at a local gym as well, if only to be inspired by the tight, young bodies around me. But when the harsh weather hits, I just flip on the big-screen TV and run on the elliptical while I jot down notes as ideas come to me.

As I age, I have to work harder to keep my body in shape. I've always been tall and thin and over the past decade, muscular, and intend to keep myself that way. Straining under the weights or jumping up and down in aerobics class reminds me that I'm alive. In fact, I'm very strong when I have to be.

My lust is the only thing that tears me away from my experiments. I can go for long periods of time, deep in the throes of my research, without an erotic thought, but then out of nowhere I'll get the urge to hunt. To prowl through the darkest of clubs and experience whatever sensory delights I can gorge on.

Sight, sound, smell, taste, feel—all of them need to be satiated and I know various places where I can feast on such decadence.


Despite my many accolades and my lust-hunting adventures, I still have stretches of immense loneliness.

The few men and women I did try to connect with, the few experiments I did conduct did not yield the results that I had hoped.

It seemed pointless and time consuming to go through night after night of chitchatting with various men and women in hopes of finding a common ground to base some kind of existence on. I had mental equality with my peers at the university; however, as I mentioned, those liaisons were never worth the while.

Sex clubs and fetish clubs with their anonymous bodies, don't-ask, don't-tell and high-level locked-lipped secrecy did their duty in keeping my appetites fulfilled, and my work consumed most of the rest of my days.

Loneliness aches through me.

I wonder why, after so many nights in sex clubs trying many wild and exotic things with the most beautiful men and women in the city—no, the province—that I still think about Specimen 1 and our stolen moments at the party.

*Specimen 2*

It was one of those times to act out my decadence. The days of concocting formulas and revising my experiments had taken their toll and the loneliness crept in. Over the past few years, there have been a plethora of alternative lifestyle clubs popping up all over the country. I'm lucky enough to live not far from one of the hottest in our city. After years of yearning, anxiety and trepidation, I finally started to attend and found that a single woman of any age seems to be quite welcome. I don't go very often, but when I do go, I tend to have a good time and get my business done.

I hit the sex club the other day. By the middle of the night, I found myself in an orgy. A familiar place. A comfortable place. It was a decadent delight of multiple bodies entwining with each other. All around me, the rooms and beds and alcoves were filled with the writhing bodies and guttural moans of people in deep, perverse pleasure.

On my way back from the bathroom, I followed some guy up the stairs back to my threesome bed and marveled at the tattoos on his slender yet muscular calves. In the dim light I couldn't quite make out what they were, but I gazed pleasingly up his tight, toned body and saw more ink on his arms and back.

He turned out to be the guy in the bed next to me and while I continued on with the dudes I had left, I couldn't help but stare at the brown-haired, tattooed guy and his lady lover.

As one of the young, buff men I was playing with fucked me, I thought about how there seemed to be an abundance of hunky tattooed boys in the club that night. My libido hit overdrive.

I stared at one tattooed guy. He caught me watching him and grinned back at me, not missing a stroke with his lovely lady.

"Hi," I said to him while pinned under my lover.

He reached out to touch me. As he slid out from his lady, he pressed his lips against mine. We kissed and his lady kissed the stranger I was already fucking. The four of us entwined into and around each other, hands roaming and touching, continuously copulating.

Eventually, to my lusty surprise, I ended up fucking tattooed guy and my, oh my, he took me to the moon and back without missing a beat. I found out later that he was a triathlete, so that explained the stamina.

"You're so big," I moaned into his neck as he entered me. "Oh my God."

"Mmmm, you're delicious," he replied as he pushed into me. He filled my void magnificently for an hour, two hours. We rocked together on the mattresses, thoughts of other lovers leaving our minds. His tightly toned arms were a pleasure to stroke; his firm ass was a joy to squeeze. I let him take me in the missionary position for a long time and then I climbed on top of him, difficult to perch with his magnificent length. I was able to maneuver an angle that created delicious friction for both of us. I rubbed against him, finding delight in his taste and smell.

When the lights snapped on in the club, a great disappointment filled me.

I didn't want the night to end. I didn't want him to leave my body. He seemed like the yin to my yang, the way his body complemented mine, the way he seemed to know exactly when to pull my hair and hold me down. He also didn't complain when I flipped around and pinned him down, holding his hands behind his head while grinding on top of him.

I gave him my number. When he called the next day, I dropped all that I was doing, and we hit the club again. It was the first time I'd gone into the club with an actual date and we wandered around all night, watching and fucking, and fucking and watching.

There's something in his deep-brown eyes that I want to know, that I need to know.

His stamina is something that I don't think I've seen before, or at least, haven't experienced for a very long time.

*Journal*

The two tattooed guys, the blond and the brunet, weigh heavily on my mind.

Specimen 1, the blond author, lives so far away that I can only enjoy him by staring at his pictures or playing with him on the webcam. I ache to feel him inside of me again, to hear his accent in my ear, to feel the brush of his lips against my neck.

Specimen 2, the brunet, is always busy. Likely avoiding me but that just makes the challenge more interesting. We all have our finish lines to cross.

My lust for my two young men only inspires me to work harder at my experiments. I need to calculate the exact formula this time. No more room for errors.

If I could only freeze-frame those exquisite moments in time, those wondrous seconds where my boys brought me to mind-blowing ecstasy and, I would hope, they brought themselves as well. If only a human could live in that moment forever, suspended in pleasure indefinitely, there would be no more pain and loneliness. There would be no more sorrow. No more agonizing anticipation or clumsy games. There would only be exhilaration and ecstasy. For all of us.

*Specimen 2*

We finally hooked up again and it wasn't the same.

But how could it be?

Daylight and sobriety were not a winning combination.

He showed me the bikes he had mounted on his apartment walls, that he used to race in triathlons.

"I've decided to stop going to the club," he told me, stroking the wheel of his bike.

"Who needs the club?" I asked him, stepping close to him. This time I wore black heels and I easily towered four inches over the tiny little athlete.

"I'm training for my next race. So I have to eat on a certain schedule and sleep a lot. I get up when you bar party people are just going to bed."

"Well, that doesn't work so well, does it?" I asked, trying to touch him but he skittered out of reach like a frightened rabbit.

I returned to the couch, watching him with amusement as he turned to face me.

"These races, they take a lot of time," he said.

"That's okay. I'm here now, you're here now..." I patted the couch.

He sat down and was shy as he touched my leg.

"Who are we kidding?" I asked him as I led him to his room.

He was bigger and more magnificent than I had remembered through a drunken haze at the bar. However, my sober self had a bit of trouble receiving him. We fumbled around a bit, and though all I had to do was straddle him a certain way, he was too young, and dare I say, cocky, to let me be in charge.

He grew impatient and soon there was blood on the sheets. Of course, blood doesn't bother me, but he grew pale and excused himself to the bathroom. He turned on the shower and soon I joined him.

He was pensive and hesitant in the shower. His youth didn't give him enough experience with bleeding women. Periods. Virginity. Menopause. Big dicks in tiny holes. Women bleed. It's life. He'll learn. And, quite frankly, I'm sure I'm not the first woman to bleed over that big dick, but likely the first to follow him on his sucky fit into the shower.

The mood was lost, no matter how I coaxed him. I grew frustrated with his immaturity and finally called it a day.

By the time I left, I felt like he couldn't get rid of me fast enough. Poor boy. He just couldn't replicate the easygoing fun that the club offered. But that's okay. I remember the flashing lights and booming music while a tattooed triathlete with a big dick fucked the shit out of me. I'll find that moment again.

The calculations went better this evening. Progress is being made.

*Journal*

The formulas appear to work. The results of the latest trial run have been computed and all appears to be in order. But I'm not quite ready to conduct my real experiments just yet.

There are many other types of preparations that need attention.

In the meantime, I dream. I dream of the three muses of beauty, intelligence and stamina who keep me inspired. I dream of the day when I can gaze upon my lovers daily and draw strength from their vibrancy and motivation. I dream of embracing youth and ambition while it is still fresh, before life sours it.

I found intelligence.

I found stamina.

I know it won't be long before I find beauty. Beauty is all around me, which is what makes this last choice so difficult. I need a beauty who leaves me breathless. A unique vision who won't bore me.

*Specimen 3*

If there is a goddess on earth, I found her, too, at the sex club. Tall, slender, her flesh a coppery brown, perfectly shaped from her shoulders to her round, firm ass. She was walking around in nothing but stilettos and a giant butterfly painted in latex across her breasts. Her perfect nipples were round hard buttons that barely moved when she walked—no, strutted—around the club. Her heels were so high that when I was introduced to her I couldn't help but lick the nipple that was inches from my mouth. It was just as well because I was tongue-tied for once.

I met the older man she was with and we politely shook hands. He cast me a cold stare. I knew that a threesome would be out with them. He was looking for a young, tight unicorn. I was too old for his barometer.

The beauty and I were ships that passed in the night, but I'll never forget her glowing green eyes and angelic face.

I watched her glide around the room, kissing men and women alike as her lecherous date looked on. She smiled at me often. At last, she kissed a girl and the old man liked it. They disappeared to a private room and I never saw her again.

The bartender told me she's a model from California and gave me a name. I Googled her immediately when I got home that night.

Her online portfolio is magnificent. She will be a stunning addition to my experiment.

*Journal*

I'm not sure what I'm waiting for. I've picked my three lusts—the beauty, the artist and the jock.

The preparations are ready. The final touches were finished this morning and the house has been prepared. The laboratory is ready. All the software has been updated and devices checked and rechecked.

A thrill surges through me as I contemplate my newest experiment. In celebration, I watched my copy of *Human Centipede* again and drank far too much red wine. I decided to make it a double-feature, science-fiction movie night and put on *Rocky Horror Picture Show* and jumped around to the "Time Warp". So now I will go rest. There are very busy days ahead.

*Specimen 1*

I lured him for a visit by promising to take him to the sex club, which I did. He had a marvelous time in the orgies, as did I, watching his beautiful body fuck women crying out at the size of his cock, as well as taking him deep inside of me myself.

We had a wonderful long weekend and he greatly enjoyed the MP3 I gave him.

*Specimen 2*

Though he sends little poke emails as if to see if I'm still alive, I'm not sure if he's interested or not. I figured he must have a girlfriend and screws around on the side. Otherwise, why be so weirdly evasive? I waited to see him race in one of the local triathlons. He was surprised to see me at the finish line, especially when he was surrounded by what seemed like quite the tight, firm little cheerleading squad. But I just smiled and gave him a special type of MP3 that he could wear in one ear like a Bluetooth and change music tracks with the click of a tiny button on the side of it. He seemed pleased with his new toy as I watched him walk away with his blonde, athletically young harem.

*Specimen 1*

Specimen 1 had been packing his suitcase when I entered his bedroom. He looked almost dwarfed by the looming four-poster, mahogany canopy king bed where his suitcase lay on top of the mattress, clothes neatly folded all around it. Wooden gargoyles leered from the top of the burgundy velvet canopy, watching his every move. I wore one of my long white lab coats, stuffed full of necessary equipment. Other than little black panties and my heels, I wore nothing else under it.

The way he looked at me, that brief hesitation, I knew he saw something in my face, my eyes that he didn't quite like. He expected me to be upset and was bracing himself for it as he planted the folded squares of clothes into the rectangular suitcase.

"Leaving so soon?" I asked. "This is most unexpected."

"I have a book deadline. I have to get going. These books don't write themselves," he half grinned.

He patted his clothes one last time and then clicked shut his suitcase.

"When do you think you'll make it back this way?" I asked him. "The door is always open."

"I'm not sure… These books. Three-book deal. It's a lot, you know? I've never had this big of a contract before."

"I see." As I realized that my lips had tightened, my nerves stretched to shining, shimmering threads quivering as delicately as spiderwebs, I forced a smile. I forced a relaxed drop to my face, a full-lip pout as I kissed his shoulder. Composure was key as I donned my mask of seduction.

"Miriam," he said, tilting my face up towards his. I stared into his sad blue eyes. "I have to go write my book. I'll be back. I just don't know when."

He touched his lips to mine, a brush as strangers.

"You can work here. I have everything you need. You wouldn't have to worry about anything but writing. I have my own experiments to conduct."

"I need to get back."

"But you're not scheduled to leave today. Your ticket…"

"I'm sorry. I changed the ticket without telling you. I have the muse. It's urging my return. I need to get this done. I'm sorry." His voice cracked, that soft, lilting accent turning average words into something more decorative. I understood his urge to get to his project. I most certainly did. But what I had to offer was better. A beautiful office, no worry about paying rent, and no responsibilities but writing and pleasing me.

He likely didn't understand how alone he was really going to be once I started the family-building process.

"Please, stay, Scott," I said. I ran my hands down his arms and then up to his face. I cupped his face so that he had to look into my eyes. I wore my violet contacts and knew they were disarming him with their vibrancy.

"You wouldn't have to lift a finger. Endless food and booze. Endless time to write. No worry about anything but enjoying me once in a while."

"It's not the same, Miriam. I need to be home with my muse."

His words cut me to the core as if he'd used a knife. There was someone else. Someone he'd kept hidden from me.

"Who's your muse?"

Scott sighed and flung his arms up. "You know. The muse. Creativity. Demon. Goddess. Pandora. Lilith. Medusa. She's whoever you want her to be."

Is this what it's like to be an artist? I've heard about these muses before but I still don't understand them.

"So you're not living with a woman?"

Scott laughed. "Hell no, Miriam. I'm not a bloody asshole, you know. Give me some credit…coming here with you." He hugged me into his arms from behind and pecked at my neck. I laughed although it didn't tickle. Over the years, I've observed other women laughing when their necks are tickled. I've never really understood the tickling thing and wonder if maybe I was born with something missing. However, it's easier to feign the sensation in order to please him than to encourage his disdain and thus provide a reason to leave too soon.

I kissed him back and for a moment it seemed that I had won. His warmth traveled through my mouth and into my bones. For a little while I was under his spell, believing that he would stay. But when our lips parted, he turned away. Before I knew it, he was back to his prissy packing-and-running-away plan. My solar plexus twinged and a knot grew in my belly. There was someone else, eagerly waiting to feel his embrace. She may not live with him but her tug on his attention was real.

I watched him go through his last round of packing and fidgeting, checking buckles and double patting down shirts. I grinned a little, which made him nervous, my hands thrust deep into my lab coat pockets, tapping the bottles.

I didn't get mad.

Well, at least on the outside.

Inside I was screaming in a rage akin to Eminem's early rants. My Superman is not leaving, he's not dead, he's not off to save the world. He's going to stay right here and do what he's meant to do.

Specimen 1's eyes were leery, sad as always and filled with that distant look guys get when they are done with you. But I wasn't done with him. I slid my hands from my pockets and ran them down my thighs. The dance had only just begun.

Tearing my panties out from under my lab coat, I held them up like a trophy before his face. Before he could make a sound, I pushed him back onto the bed.

"Miriam, the plane..." he stammered as I snapped open his jeans.

"We'll be done before you're finished complaining." I grinned as I saw he wasn't wearing underwear and wasn't nearly as unenthusiastic as he pretended to be. I straddled him, unbuttoning my lab coat and holding the material away from his face. When I leaned over to kiss him, my body clenching against his as he thrust into me, I stabbed him in the neck with a hypodermic needle I had slipped from my pocket.

He didn't have much reaction time, but the sudden rush of something different through his system released him into some kind of orgasm. He cried out and then collapsed, his eyes shut. I finished pleasing myself, smelling his delicious scent and holding his limp torso against mine. I trembled with the eagerness of a puppy smelling the dinner bowl being lowered to her face.

My body had a will of its own, craving his familiarity, my nose filled with the smell of his brilliance, my senses tingling and quivering like an overtight E string on a violin. The release I finally experienced was the best we'd had together yet.


It took a few minutes to undress him fully. First I pulled him from the bed and onto the floor. Buttons and limbs and his lifeless weight made all those gym sessions pay off. I rolled him back and forth, careful not to knock his precious head into the clawed feet of the bed. Once he was naked, I left him curled up on the floor in rescue position.

The bed needed to be fitted with plastic sheets. I was sweaty and they kept sticking to my fingers, but at last I wrestled them onto the mattress. Then I layered two more giant loose strips of plastic across the bed, taping them with everyone's favorite choice of adhesive.

I rolled over several shiny metal trays from behind the curtains. Earlier I had stocked them with various instruments and serums. I opened a panel hidden in the wallpaper and flicked a switch. Large, bright overhead lights in the room flashed on. I walked around the room and inspected the hidden cameras I'd strategically placed in random spots, to make sure they were running.

After carefully inspecting the trays and recording all my scientific findings into the other journal, I was ready to begin. My temples throbbed with the anticipation of a new beginning. Experiment 698 would be my victory. Sweat poured down my forehead as I counted and recounted the serum dosages ready to be administered through the hypodermic needles laying on the tray, recording the EMFs in the tiny implants, inspecting connections and computer codes one last time.

There could be no failure this time. Everything has been prepared and double-checked an infinite number of times. There are curves to be adjusted for each individual, but 698 overall will be the one that will succeed.

It was tough work, but I heaved Specimen 1 back onto the bed. I had to get him on there with the minimum amount of stress, so I rolled in one of my stretchers from the lab. I slid him onto the stretcher then raised it to the height of the bed and rolled him over onto the plastic-clad bed.

That was one good reason I continued to go to the gym. I had to be able to lift heavy bodies quickly and safely. He wasn't going to be asleep forever.

I shackled him to the bedposts by the ankles and wrists. Once he was tightly secured, I put a ball gag into his mouth.

He was a lovely vision, all bound up like that, his tattoos wound around his arms, across his chest, splashes of color painting his beautiful young body. I ran my pen down his flesh, marking the spots where the implants would go.

Although his skin twitched as if he was tickled, I knew his mind was asleep, regardless of what sensations his body could and could not feel.

Before I began my surgery, I rolled over the electrocardiogram machine and applied all the electrodes to him. The tape rolled out so I could consult it quickly and easily, instead of scrolling through yet another monitor.

I put the headphones on his ears and began to play the important recordings.

Once I had him hooked up to an IV and heart machine and oxygen, I began my surgery.

By all observations, the sedative had been the appropriate dosage. He barely flinched when I opened his flesh with tiny cuts with my scalpel.

Into each cut was placed a small electromagnetic device the size of a grain of rice. The diagram of the placements is in the experiment journal. They were inserted head to toe. These devices were the newest component to my experiment. I had observed resistance to just audio exposure and drug exposure, but the newest phase was this particular model of implants.

My vinyl gloves were slick with his blood by the time I finished. I'm more of a brainiac than a surgeon. Vinyl is hard to control but latex induces hives and rashes on my skin.

My nerves continued to be frazzled from preparing him for surgery and some of the cuts were a bit deeper than I'd intended. The process had been sped up, which hadn't been factored in. There had been no time to develop full concentration as he had taken me by surprise. He wasn't due to leave for two more days, so something must have happened. Something happened to alert or alarm him.

I can't take any chances. Couldn't take any chances. Won't take any chances. I had him here and who knew if I could entice him of his own free will to return again.

It had to be now or never.

My adrenaline was high as I wiped the blood from Specimen 1. A bowl of warm water and a soft dabbing cloth were all that were necessary. I carefully inspected each site for possibility of tear or infection. It was evident that once he was healed from the little cuts, no one, including him, would believe that there were implants in every site.

I washed him head to toe in a second sponge bath. This one contained antiseptics and numbing gels. He was so still throughout the process that others might have thought him dead. His chest barely rose, a gentle snort emitting from his nose every so often to show that he still indeed lived. His manhood remained impressive, even in repose. I inspected my work along his genitalia and was satisfied that he wouldn't feel the implants, no matter how much he might play with himself.

I used several rolls of paper towels attempting to get rid of blood and water and any other dripping, seeping liquids.


He is sleeping on the bed while I sit in a chair across from him, documenting my clinical observations in one journal while recording my random thoughts in another.

After I cleaned his wounds yet again, it was clear that his scars would be no bigger than freckles and they were placed discreetly when possible. I didn't want to mar such a beautiful man with more mutilation than absolutely necessary. Although he could always get more lovely tattoos.

I stripped the plastic from the bed, rolling his body first one way and then another, careful not to spill more blood than necessary. It was grueling, careful work, trying not to break open his wounds nor wake him though he was chained hand and foot to the bed with sticky sheets of plastic clinging to him.

It was during times such as these that I'm grateful for air-conditioning, but I was still sweating despite the refreshing coolness. I even stopped at one point and dragged two fans in from the gym upstairs.

Once the room was restored back to a bedroom from an operating room, I breathed a sigh of relief. The bright lights were gone, surgery equipment returned to the lab, fans returned to the gym, Specimen 1 sleeping in his handcuffs as if it were just another night at the fetish club.

The future looked bright indeed.

*Specimen 1*

I was going to let him stay awake today. He was calm and peaceful and seemed very happy to see me. He had no concept of time or days and didn't seem worried that a week had passed. At least those were my hopeful observations as I approached him. I hoped that the dosage wasn't too high and making him stupid. I couldn't bear a stupid writer.

"Oh, you're awake," I smiled as I approached him. He blinked at me several times and tried to speak. His voice was crackly. His sad eyes watched me with confusion.

"You're just thirsty, darling," I said to him. I poured him a cup of water. As he tried to reach for it, he realized he was cuffed.

"What the fuck?" he yelled as sudden strength flooded him and he struggled against his shackles.

"It's okay. You had a bad trip, that's all," I soothed as I opened a nightstand drawer.

"You've kidnapped me, that's what you've done." He was flailing wildly, chains clanking as he fought the restraints.

"Scott, relax, we were playing bondage games and you passed out," I said as I approached him, holding a syringe behind my back.

"Why the hell would I pass out?" His yanking at the shackles was distracting, which worked in my favor.

"Because you've been taking some really good drugs, my beautiful writer." I leaned over to lick his ear. As he reacted to my obvious seduction, I plunged the needle into his arm and pumped the serum into him.

"Fucking bitch," he screamed, flailing around anew, but only for about six seconds before he passed out once more.

The effects of the drugs would finally wear off and he'd be back to his brilliant, calculating lothario self once more.

He hopefully would not remember the week of restraint and therefore I would hopefully not have to answer for it. The calculations indicate that his memory patterns won't include waking and sleeping cycles that occur during this week.

I pushed a few buttons on the various devices, recorded my findings in the other journal, did a memory dump from the computers to an external hard drive I keep in one of my safes. The batteries in the security camera were also replaced.

I would have to wait another day to begin the reconditioning when he wasn't so angry.

In glancing at his cell phone the previous week, there were no apparent texts or photos of over women. However, once I connected his cell phone to my computer, a specific program could extract all of his data, even everything he had ever erased.

I'd had this program for cell phone extraction created for me by a previous specimen, before the serum consumed him and he died of a heart attack. It was tragic but I've always appreciated this program he created just for me to hack into cell phones. A lovely gift. I don't often get much back from my specimens in the way of gifts. So he remains dear to my heart, Specimen 5 from Experiment 691.

There is indeed a girl in Specimen 1's hometown. I sent a few texts her way through my program and that problem should be solved. He'll never know that she contacted him or that he told her he doesn't want to see her anymore, that he's going to Europe for six months to be a writer in residence. She did try to plead with him not to go, even called him, and I used my voice-modulator software to emulate his voice and told her myself, as Scott, that she was to never call again.

Specimen 1 can have no distractions. He has books to write and a family to build.

*Specimen 1*

Four days slipped by as he straddled the worlds, healing and learning. The next time he woke in my presence, he was docile.

"Dr. Miriam, I presume," he joked half-heartedly. I locked the bedroom door behind me though I had no fear of his escape. This house, the rooms, were a cell within a cell within a cell. There was no escape for any man, woman or child if I chose it to be that way. Grant money is a wonderful thing.

"How do you feel?" I asked him.

"Stiff. Do I have to stay in here forever? I don't remember my safe word anymore," he said.

"I'll let you out, my dear," I said as I unlocked the shackles. He sat up with a groan, rubbing his wrists and ankles.

"I need the bathroom," he said.

"Go ahead."

He slowly pulled himself from the bed and steadied himself to walk. I helped him along, inspecting his wounds visually for signs of infection or tearing. Most of them were invisible at this point. Young flesh healed nicely, thanks to the daily vitamin injections and holistic lotions I rubbed on him.

I let him navigate the bathroom on his own. There was no need to fear his escape from there, it didn't go anywhere. And there was nothing he could use as a weapon against me upon his return. Besides, he was naked, so there was no place to hide anything at all.

When he returned from the bathroom, he was fully aroused, his eyes glassy and full of lust.

"How about it, Doctor?" he asked as he pushed me back on the bed. Before I could speak, his hands were clasping mine against the sheets. He kneed my legs apart, staring into my eyes as he filled me up with a couple of weeks of wet dreams.

When he was finished, he crawled back into bed and slept for another two days. I still had to shackle him; there was no reason to trust him just yet. The need for a ball gag was apparent as well, even though this room, each floor and the entire house has layers of soundproofing materials. Nosy neighbors have already thwarted too much of my past.

*Journal*

The pattern continued in a predictable two-day cycle over the course of two more weeks. Specimen 1 would wake up, desire one vigorous round of intercourse and then drop back to sleep for another three days. More detailed notes regarding his vital signs and other particulars during this period can be found in the formal journals and logs.

Quite simply, I decided to adjust the serum formulas. The buzzing of the electrodes invaded the silence of the night or at least added a layer over the hum of machines and the furnace. The daily regime of programming the implants could be tedious and any way to add fun to the task is always embraced. In the darkness, the faint glow of the electrodes is almost discernible when I wear custom infrared magnifying glasses that I designed myself a few years ago. Deciphering the data would be easier upon later review if it was more accurate.

As much as I enjoyed the easy convenience of Specimen 1's behavior while he slept for days, that pattern of sleep and sex wasn't quite the arrangement I had in mind when I first proceeded with this experiment. It wasn't healthy for an intelligent man like him to be reduced to sleeping and fornicating. He needed to stretch his mind further than two instinctual places. He needed to interact in his dark world of literature—dance with words, wrestle with concepts, create creatures who performed his own bidding.

As master of his own universe, he will fit nicely into the world I'm creating. The family starts with him.

He woke and saw me standing in the doorway, watching him. I grinned and approached him. He shrugged his shoulders and gave me a puppy-dog-eyes stare.

"Would you like me to remove your ball gag?" I asked him. He nodded. I hovered for a moment, enjoying his look of expectation, fully expecting it to turn to spewing rage the minute the ball came out.

I wiped the spittle from his chin while he worked his jaw.

"Better?" I asked.

"Much. Thank you, love," he said.

"Are you tired of the shackles?"

"You bet. I promise to behave if you let me loose."

"You will behave. Of that I've no doubt." I produced the keys to the handcuffs and leg cuffs, and proceeded to set him free. Much as other times, the first thing he did was head for the bathroom. This time, I heard the shower. I crossed my fingers and hoped against hope that he was finally closer to himself by now. It was a good time to test how well I placed the implants and if they had been embedded deep enough into his body. Now that he is in the process of being reprogrammed, the voltage is much higher. Getting them wet might create a short or a boost, and could cause a stroke, shock or death.

He emerged from the shower, happy and horny. The implants were safe. He lay me back on the bed and had his way with me. This time, when we were finished, his curiosity was piqued.

"Why am I here?" he asked as he held me in his arms.

"I can help you. Not only will you be renowned in the egghead circles but I have connections to blow your mass-market career wide open."

"And what do I do in return?"

"Just write your books. Consider me a patron of the arts. Why should the government care where parts of grants go if it's to encourage an art form? I'll take care of you. At least let me try."

"Maybe I should follow your advice for a while," he said. "I'm not getting anything done the way we're going right now."

I gave him a journal to write in by pen, as I do with this one. I also gave him a laptop with no current Internet connection just yet. He could use it while he was shackled in bed, I'd keep the chains loose enough to type.

That day, I allowed him to sit at the huge oak desk I had built especially for him in his very own office. There were hundreds of books in the glass-windowed mahogany cases that stretched to the ceiling. His office was everything I'd cobbled together about what a writer might enjoy. His own book covers framed in intricately carved mahogany, along with framed pictures and news articles I'd blown up from webzines.

He was a bit groggy as he sat in the plus-sized leather executive chair. He looked around the room.

"This is lovely."

"If anything is missing, let me know. I'll get it for you."

"I'll let you know."

He opened up the laptop and began to write. The steady tapping of his keys excited me and I left him alone. From my office on the second floor, I had a dashboard of over 150 cameras that were monitoring the house. There were three large master monitors on which I could watch something in particular while I was working.

I observed him typing and stopping. He got up and walked around the room, looking at the books, opening up one or two and smiling as he read brief passages before replacing them. He went over to the bar. It was already stocked for him. Everything was watered down to a specific level so that he wouldn't overdose with the serums.

All the calculations are recorded in the other books.

He poured himself a glass of scotch and was pleasantly surprised to see ice in the ice bucket when he opened the lid. He looked around the room and it appears he spotted the camera. He stared right into the camera and raising his glass, mouthed the words *thank you.*

It can't hurt for him to know he's being watched, I guess. He's not exactly a pushover.

But at bedtime, I administered his medication and put him back into his shackles and ball gag.

He seems a bit frazzled, a bit out of sorts, but I think once he's spent a couple of days writing and escaping into his dreamworlds, he'll feel better.


*Specimen 1*

He likes his new office. He sits there day after day, working on his book and playing on Facebook.

Well, he thinks he's on Facebook. He's really inside a shell that replicates Facebook, but he's actually interacting with bots. I control everything that goes on in his Facebook world. He can chat with whomever he desires because in the end, it's just me and my bots. Any plans to escape or cheat would be easily thwarted.

On Facebook, he believes he will see his lover once more. They have been making secret plans. Except, he's been making plans with me.

In all honesty, his notes to ladylove have become less frequent and leaning towards complacency. He's focusing more on his new book and less on networking as his first deadline draws near.

His complacency towards ladylove and his growing dependence on me are partly accomplished by the implants. I've nearly weaned him from the serums, now it will be just an electrical matter.

When he's not writing to his heart's content, he's fucking my brains out on his king-sized bed in the basement apartment I furnished for him. The more he writes, the better the sex. That's something I hadn't anticipated and is a lovely side effect.

*Specimen 1*

There came a point where I began to take him out in public.

It began very carefully one day. He was shackled to the bed. I had ratcheted the chains tightly so that his hands were above his head. Not painfully so, but enough. His legs were tight, not a hope he could move a muscle. I couldn't have him flinching.

"You're getting very pale, my darling. You need some vitamin D. Sunshine," I told him.

He couldn't answer with the ball gag firmly in place. I didn't want his chatter to distract from the seriousness of this next step.

"I want to take you out, but you must always wear this."

He turned his head to watch me go to one of his dresser drawers and produce a type of male chastity belt. I slid the leather strap under his hips. I had it designed so that it buckled at the sides, not at the back. I slipped his cock through a metal hole then tightened it with a spring-action hook.

"Now, none of this should actually hurt at all. Am I right?"

He shifted his hips around and nodded in agreement that he didn't feel any pain.

"However, you try to say anything to anyone or make any false moves and something like this will happen."

I retrieved a remote control from one of the metal trays. I turned it to a very low level. His eyes widened and then he relaxed as he began to fall into the lull of a soothing buzz around his scrotum.

"You feel that? Good. Remember, I can make that buzzing feel really good for you, as it does on the lowest level, or I can turn the dial up to ten where your skin will actually burn and your testicles will cook within one minute. Do we understand each other?"

He nodded.

I turned the vibrations off and put the remote in my pocket. Unknown to him, I had a keypad implanted in the bracelet that I wore. It contained programming not only for the belt but for all of his implants as well. He could explode into one big gooey mess should he try to escape. It was enough to threaten him with his balls cooking.

Our first outing was to a grocery store and all went well. He behaved beautifully, being very polite to strangers and patient with the whole shopping experience.

Our second outing was to a pub. That went very well too. There came a point where I even brought him to faculty parties. He never left my side, his eyes never strayed to another woman and he never made signals for help.

This was good.

I took him to one of my boring faculty cocktail parties. This one was to honor a scientist who was working with monkeys and THC. Specimen 1 behaved beautifully. He even seemed to thrive under the recognition he received from admirers of his books and the lecture he had given that day so long ago.

"Dr. Miriam, we rarely see you at these anymore," Dr. Williams, the crusty old chairman of the board said to me while eyeing Specimen 1.

"I've been quite busy with my experiments and, of course, showing Mr. Gravenhurst the wonderful sights and delights of our city."

"So it would seem. You are looking well, so you're obviously doing something right," he quipped as he wandered off to the next guest.

I'm satisfied this experiment is going well.


*Specimen 1*

His accent sends shivers of delight through me, the way his foreign tongue twists words brings even one of my dry medical textbooks alive. I've declared that every now and again he'll read me some of his works in progress. I sit back on his king-sized bed while he sits naked at my feet, reading a few pages from his latest creepy creations. The lilt of his voice, the way he pronounces his words, the look of concentration on his handsome face while he reads his work to me—all make me wet with gleeful anticipation.

I've grown to trust Specimen 1. He has settled into his life with me, takes orders and is compliant. Even his Facebook messages to his lady friend have stopped. He wrote to her to tell her he's not coming back, that he's happy working on his books in lavish surroundings.

Specimen 1 doesn't need to be shackled anymore.

Of course, the house is on lockdown, there is no way for him to escape or even contact the outside world.

He can sleep freely in his bed now, with no chains, no ball gag to hinder his rest. He wakes when he desires and sleeps when he desires.

He is adjusting perfectly.


*Specimen 3*

When I went to the sex club last night with Specimen 1, I asked about her, the goddess. Surprisingly, the doorman gave me her email address.

Today I emailed her and after we went back and forth a couple of times, I told her I wanted to send her a present. She sent me an address.

I packaged up a state-of-the-art MP3 player that looks like an earring and is clipped to the ear. There are actually two of them that look like pretty rhinestones but also provide surround sound between them.

I hope she enjoys her present.


*Specimen 1*

My calculations were way off. I weaned him from the serums too quickly and too soon. I was premature in granting him so much freedom. I was nearly defeated by my own enthusiasm.

I was sleeping in my own bedroom on the second floor when the door creaked open. The sound startled me awake, and, more so, I was knocked off guard when a pillow was slammed down on my face.

It took a moment for me to register what was going on. But once I shook off the slippery tendrils of dreams and faced my reality, I was ready. My gym training at work once more, I lurched into a flip, knocking the intruder back. He stumbled, fell over a chair, and then scrambled to his feet as I stood in a classic fighting stance on top of my bed.

"Who is it?" I called out. As my eyes adjusted to the dimness of the room, I saw him on the other side of the room, panting heavily, a solid figure in the shadows. He rubbed his arms, clearly surprised at my strength.

"Why are you keeping me here?" Specimen 1 asked.

"I'm not keeping you here," I said, not letting my stance drop.

"Yes, you're keeping me a prisoner. The doors are locked. The phones don't work. Even the Internet isn't the Internet."

"My, you've been busy in your explorations."

"What do you expect, Miriam? I want to go home."

The words were like a punch to my stomach. I crawled down from the bed and stood by my nightstand. I had ready-to-use hypodermic needles in there should it become necessary.

"Aren't you happy here?" I asked. "I give you everything."

"No you don't. You don't give me freedom. I'm locked in this torture chamber like something out of a Jack Ketchum novel, with my dick trussed up like a turkey if you dare let me accompany you somewhere."

"It's not like that at all, Scott. You're just tired and overreacting."

"You kept me in chains like a monster. I'm just a writer. What do you want with me?"

"I think you have an overactive imagination. I'm enjoying you as my houseguest. Don't I give you everything you desire?"

"I desire to go home. I have a deadline."

"You've been writing. I've seen you."

"But I need my notes and the other work I've written. I don't want to write from scratch the bits I've already completed. And I only have a few months left to hit my deadline."

"What notes do you need? Don't you have them with you?"

"I…"

"Don't lie to me, Scott. I can tell when you're lying." I was brave to speak to him like that. Certainly I could surmise by his body language, but in the darkness the other cues were not as obvious as they are in the daylight.

He stood, wavering, his shadow already resigned to his fate. I slipped on my bracelet that controlled the implants just in case I needed to use it. With my back to him, I eked open the nightstand table so that my weapons were ready.

"Okay, you're right. I brought my flash drive of notes with me."

"See? I knew you were too clever to travel without all you need."

I grinned in the darkness. I relaxed my stance and sat down on the bed. I patted it.

"Let's not fight, Scott. I didn't bring you here to fight with me."

As he approached me, his eyes caught the glint of distant light and their sparkle caught me off guard. A flash of blue in the darkness was startling. He sat beside me and I reached for him. We kissed and though I wanted to melt into his arms, my senses were on high alert.

His kisses grew rough and he wrestled me onto my back. His hands slipped around my neck, attempting to press his thumbs against my windpipe.

I made a note in my head to adjust the frequencies to reflect his genetic anger issues so that he couldn't be violent with his outbursts anymore.

Again those gym kickboxing classes paid off as I snapped his arms from me with my hands and kicked him away with my feet. Springing from the bed, he followed, his breath loud with the chase. I circled the room, him jumping from bed to chair to stalk me. I backed against my nightstand, my fingers slipping inside to grab one of the glass tubes. As he lunged towards me, I stuck the hypodermic needle into his chest. He flailed with me for a second or two, growing weaker as the drug ran through him.

"Bitch…" he spat as he collapsed onto the floor.

As I dragged him back to the lab, wrapping him in a blanket and padding his head with a pillow so as not to damage his beautiful brain, I mused over the fact that he came to kill me, instead of just escaping when I wasn't looking. Certainly, he could escape if he truly wanted to. There must be something I'd forgotten to close or lock in my fortress—there's always a fatal flaw. Especially in the daytime, when I often left the house without him. I found it most curious and wondered if it might be because the implant was working in the sense that he had desire for me, but it was a desire to kill me, not to copulate with me. I have to examine my notes and calculations before I can make the adjustments.

*Journal*

The overall process is going quite well. Preparations are constant as circumstances mutate.

I had to restrain Specimen 1 for another week. Completely under, with only his headset to listen to. No writing for him. He'll be starving for his muse and for sex when he finally wakens. And hopefully, by then, I'll have finished working the bugs out of the levels.

*Specimen 1*

At last, Specimen 1 is finally ready. One last trial run in his contained setting, and he appears to be fine. His lust for me overwhelmed him upon his awakening and it didn't take much coaxing on his part to entice me into his arms.

He was as powerful and wonderful as he had been before, with a new sense of urgency and pleasure.

He was much more docile in his manner. He even allowed me to put his chastity belt on without restraints.

"I understand my role now," he said, hanging his head as I fastened the heavy buckles to his thin hips. "I won't disappoint you this time, Doctor."

A wry grin touched my lips but I didn't let him see it. I was firm in my handling of him, he needed to know who the real master was and it wasn't him.

"Would you like to go to the pub?" I asked him.

His eyes lit up. "Yes, most certainly."

"It's a lovely day out there, we can go have a pint on the patio," I said. "Why don't you get dressed while I finish getting ready?"

I left his apartment, locking it from the outside, and went to my own bedroom. As I stood in my massive walk-in closet, I surveyed all my outfits. A nice, plain late-summer outfit for our trip to the pub would be good. We would likely run into colleagues, so I had to be certain to look presentable.

It took a few minutes but at last I wore a perky, casual orange-and-brown cotton plaid jacket with matching pencil skirt and an orange blouse. My last trip to the salon had rendered me a dark brunette, almost the same shade as the brown in the plaid. My makeup was perfection, cat's eyes and luscious lips. No solemn-doctor look today. I was brilliant in my Bettie Page finery. Even my remote bracelet looked great once I added some wooden and copper beads to the strands. While I assembled myself, I continued checking the monitor on my cell phone to survey his movements.

He didn't stray from his task at all. Shoulders shrugged in resignation, he retreated to the bathroom and washed his face. Once in a while, his hand would stray to his chastity belt, stroking the soft, supple leather, tugging at the tightly locked side buckles. He searched through the walk-in closet for clothes and found socks in the dresser drawers.

When I returned to Specimen 1's apartment, he looked magnificent. He wore a blue denim shirt that matched his eyes, jeans that bulked only slightly because of the chastity belt, and a leather biker jacket. My Jimmy Dean was all trussed up and ready to roll.

I took him for a long walk where we mused about how some of the maples had tinges of fall colors and were even beginning to drop. Remarking on how quickly the seasons pass, we collected lucky leaves that matched my outfit. We recited classic poetry to each other, daring each to add another line before one or the other was stumped. At one point, we had both forgotten a line to a sonnet but a quick Google on the cell phone got us back on track.

Sometimes our conversations about literature and poetry inspire me so much that I just want to cut open the top of his head and crawl right into his brain. If only it were possible. However, as he is now, he's a fine brain container. Handsome and quirky and, by all signs, well on his way to being tamed. Somewhat. I'm not interested in conferring with a zombie but I need to have control over him at all costs, or it will cost me my life and freedom.

"How would you like a new haircut?" I asked him.

"I'd like that. I've not had one in, how long? What day is it today?"

"It's been a while." I brushed my hand through his hair that was boyish and tangled. Although I loved the tousled young-man look, I preferred his close-cropped rebel persona.

We walked down to Bloor Street and I took him to my favorite salon. Lorel was on the desk, perched on the edge of her seat, her bright-red lips speaking into a headset while she waved me over to the podium. Lorel had been with the salon for about five years, though she acted like she'd always been there and knew everything about everyone. Nothing much got past her. She was one of those fleshy, buxom ladies with brightly colored manicures and too much cheap perfume who seemed to find a way to quickly get others to share their life stories while prattling along about her own.

It made her crazy that she couldn't get anything out of me in all these years. No doubt there were countless rumors about some of my more dubious experiments that rippled through the salon. And there were those couple of times I was wrongly accused and arrested for kidnapping and torture. Thank goodness for bureaucratic paperwork. Any experiments that should become public have already been shared, in code, during the long-winded presentations for my government grants. However, there would always be whispers that perhaps it was really true that I had kidnapped a person or two. But who can really believe people who have spent time in a mental institution? What is reality? What is fantasy?

My observations of Lorel, though, were keen. The less she knew about Specimen 1 and the nature of our relationship, the better. If I said nothing, I wasn't lying, now, was I?

"Dr. Frederick," she said, "pardon me."

Lorel concluded her conversation and turned to face us. She stared with intensity at Specimen 1.

"Who have we here today? Your nephew?" Lorel gets points for trying.

"This is my colleague, author Scott Gravenhurst."

Lorel grinned as Scott reached for her hand. She giggled and blushed as he kissed it. Her face was flushed and her intrusiveness evaporated into a pathetic puddle of flirting. It was truly like watching a sea lion eagerly barking for fish.

"Mr. Gravenhurst is in need of a haircut. He has a photo shoot coming up and I don't want him to look messy," I said sternly.

"Of course, right away." Lorel stood up, something she did whenever a man she fancied entered the salon.

Lorel walked with a loud *click-clack* of the new-style mile-high stilettos that I've seen for years at fetish clubs but could never imagine anyone wanting to wear such torturous footgear in everyday life. Perhaps Lorel would be a tamable subject. If only there was anything at all about her that pleased me.

Specimen 1 waited patiently, watching the buxom young hairdressers cut and poof and blow-dry. The salon had around twenty stations, each one like an individual pocket. Almost all of them were full. I remembered that it was Saturday, which had a different vibe than a weekday.

Lorel returned with Guy in tow. Guy was one of the original owners with his husband, Leonard. Their salon was popular with faculty, students and even some of the Rosedale crowd.

Guy would please me.

"This is Scott Gravenhurst, in dire need of a good lineup for his photo shoot."

"My..." Guy looked Specimen 1 up and down, "...you've picked yourself a nice one this time, Miriam."

"He's working on a novel and he needs to be absolutely fabulous for his book cover." I swooned. "You must make him mesmerizing so that we can see his magnificent eyes."

Specimen 1 started to laugh.

"Stop it, you're embarrassing me. Listen, mate, I just need it all gone. It's been too long."

"Whatever you desire, young man." Guy led Specimen 1 to one of the chairs. I sat in the lounge and pretended to thumb through magazines while checking my email. In reality, I was monitoring

Specimen 1 to be certain he didn't say anything he shouldn't. I took an earbud from one of the bobble lockets on my bracelet and put it in my ear. Through my phone, I was able to hear every word that was said.

Specimen 1 passed with flying colors. I didn't have to adjust any of the implants or buzz the chastity belt. We could continue our day and enjoy ourselves.

The news of me arriving at the salon with a man half my age hit Twitter less than five minutes after we left. There was even a picture one of the hairdressers had snapped and tweeted of Specimen 1's new haircut, as seen through a maze of mirrors.

This pleased me. Scott Gravenhurst was seen in public, being groomed for a photo shoot, and working on a book. Scott Gravenhurst is not missing, if anyone ever thought he was. He was just holed up with a deadline, but alive and well. After all, everything appeared perfectly normal, now, didn't it?

Our meanderings took us to a pub where I allowed him two draughts and a scotch. The man likes his drink and to deny him would be asking for more trouble than it's worth. The weather was so lovely that we took our drinks to the patio.

We watched the traffic go by, bicycles whizzing, kids on skateboards, dogs on leashes, the world so normal, so routine. Toronto is a pretty town in areas and the university neighborhoods are very mature, with large gorgeous maples, oaks and pines. As leaves and acorns dropped and drifted around us, I felt like the luckiest lady in the world. I wanted to embrace the moments while I could, for I knew from previous experiments this glorious high wasn't going to last.

I hope Specimen 1 will be with me forever. He is truly a man who touches me in so many ways that no other man has before him.

"Are you enjoying the day?" I asked him.

He nodded as he gazed up at the trees.

"I can't believe it's fall again."

"Almost fall. Almost time for another school year."

"I missed the whole summer." He sighed.

"No, it's only late August. You still have a long ways to go. With the global warming, it doesn't really snow or get cold before January anymore. I can't tell you how many green Christmases we've been having."

"Canada? Green Christmases?" he asked.

"It often snows around Halloween for some ghastly reason. Then warms up again. Actually, the reality is unpredictability. Every day is a surprise. You never know what clothes to wear from one hour to the next."

"I miss smoking," Specimen 1 suddenly blurted out.

"Smoking?"

"Yes, I smoke. I'm a smoker. I ran out of smokes a while back. Am I allowed to smoke?"

My heart beat faster and my eyes welled up. I'd totally neglected his smoking habit. In my quest for perfection, I denied him his own personal pleasure.

"Oh, Scott, my darling…I totally forgot. Of course you can smoke. Hell, I smoke too at parties and such. I wasn't even thinking. We'll buy you a carton on the walk home."

I looked around the patio and spotted a young lady who was about to light a cigarette. I stood up and approached her.

"Excuse me, ma'am, do you have any cigarettes left?" I asked.

"Half a pack. Would you like one?"

"Can I buy the rest?" I pulled a fifty-dollar bill from my pocket. "Is this enough?"

"Oh my, you don't have to do that," she said. "I don't mind giving you a couple for nothing."

"I'd like the rest of what you have and you've been most kind." I plunked the fifty-dollar bill on the table and picked up the pack. I removed one cigarette and put it on the bill. "Thank you, you're a sweetheart."

I waltzed back to the table with the cigarettes.

Specimen 1 already had taken a lighter from his pocket. He was so eager he was shaking in anticipation as he lit the cigarette I popped into his mouth.

He took a long haul and breathed it out with great pleasure.

"Ah, that's so much better. You have no idea."

"Again, I'm sorry, Scott. I wasn't trying to torture you."

He stared at me with those deep-blue eyes.

"I think you are…" he pointed at his crotch, "…but in different ways. I forgive you for the nicotine denial. You didn't know I'm a big smoker. And I guess I slept away most of the summer."

The sadness returned to his eyes as he stared off down the street.

"I don't really remember much about my previous day-to-day life. Just that I had one," he murmured. "Flashes of laughter, shadows of people who filled me with joy, and an ache of loss, but what have I lost?"

"Let's just enjoy our beer and the sunshine, shall we?" I said as I raised my pint to his, stopping his lament. He sighed and stared warily at my wrist.

"Sure." He raised his glass and touched it to mine. "To life."

We drank our pint and no sooner had we paid the bill than the book-club ladies came in. Of course, the Twitterverse works fast and someone had leaked that we were at the pub patio. Along came his middle-aged fans. It was touching.

"Scott Gravenhurst…" a tall blonde approached him with one of his hardcovers thrust out in one hand and a Birks monogrammed pen in the other, "…will you…please?"

Specimen 1 looked at me in fear, as if my hand was on the trigger, which it was, but I was more curious to see how this would play out.

"Ladies, we were just leaving; however, I'm sure Scott and I can be persuaded to stay and enjoy another pint with you for a bit as our next engagement isn't currently pressing."

I didn't have to ask twice as the ladies all flocked around Specimen 1, sighing over his good looks and having him autograph their books. Before long, everyone was settled in with more rounds of beer and Specimen 1 was regaling the ladies with his tales of himself (?) as a lad in his homeland. I had stopped drinking after two beers, but I let Specimen 1 continue on. I was curious to see how much he could drink and what he would say or do in public.

Being in the arts, it was easy for him to talk about his adventures and never comment on why he was in town at all. The ladies were enchanted and more tweets flew around the interweb.

Scott Gravenhurst is alive and well.

Too bad, spurned girlfriends, it's not the first time he's disappeared. He left his homeland under nefarious circumstances and has been state-hopping and woman-hopping ever since. Seeing his phone records showed me he was indeed the player I'd pegged him for. It must be driving him nuts to see all these women today and not be able to take their numbers for nasty sexting later.

He's playing the game well for now, but we'll see for how long. One of us will have to break at some point. It's how the game works. If he can accept that I'm the master and he's the slave then there will be no issues. However, part of his attraction is his questioning, feisty character. It's a quandary that I need to ponder and obtain more evidence to resolve.

By the time I locked the door to his apartment for the night, with no shackles, no chastity belt, just him being free, I was feeling very optimistic about the experiment. Perhaps he was trainable. Perhaps it was just an act.

Only time would truly tell.

*Specimen 2*

He emailed and said that he wanted to see me. How could I not comply? It has been months since I've seen his hot little body, his big cock, his expressive dark eyes. I told him to come to my house.

This time I wore club clothes and drank about four shots of tequila before he showed up. He was cute in his jeans and T-shirt, and rather surprised when I pounced like a tiger—or should I say cougar—onto him as I led him downstairs, beyond Specimen 1's apartment and into the wing I'd prepared for Specimen 2, which he didn't know yet.

Specimen 1 was writing in his fortress, locked in the soundproof apartment, with no knowledge of my whereabouts.

Specimen 2 entered what was going to be his apartment.

"Nice place, but why do you stay in the basement when the rest of the house is so large? Don't you sleep upstairs?"

"Yes, my bedroom is indeed upstairs. In fact, I have many bedrooms and guest suites. For me, it's a change of pace to use this room, as I've not had a chance to test out this brand-new bed yet."

The apartment was much smaller than Specimen 1's, although Specimen 2 certainly wouldn't know that. I pushed the mattress on the bed. In my mind, I was chuckling. His king-sized bed was made from wrought iron. I wanted his apartment to have a more modern, sleek feel and there were even framed pictures I had taken of him of him racing in triathlons over the past months on the walls.

He stopped to stare at the photos. He turned his head and looked at me questioningly.

"Why..."

"Why are you still wearing clothes?" I purred. "Where's that hot triathlete body I've been craving." I ran my hands along his arms, pinching him like the witch in "Hansel and Gretel"—just how much flesh was on these bones?

"Those photos..." he stammered.

"Yes, I have some photos of you. I was hoping you'd remember me one day," I said, distracting him. "After all, why adorn my walls with strangers when I personally know an agile and fit award-winning athlete?"

Specimen 2 grinned and eagerly kissed me, his hand cupping my crotch. He wasn't much of a talker, not like Specimen 1. He was focused on what he wanted and he set the pace for getting us there. The fact that I towered over him by almost a foot inspired my desire for him.

I helped him peel off his clothes. Muscles, tattoos and abs, oh my. How I'd missed his tiny, tight body and his big huge cock.

We started with him on top but it wasn't long before I overpowered him and rode my way to ecstasy. He even let me put him in handcuffs while we played. It was so easy, too easy, and that was fine. Specimen 1 was taking all my brainpower to outsmart him; it was nice to have a lower-level brain to cope with. Specimen 2 only cared about his physical agenda, without thinking through the consequences. It made his capture so much easier.

*Specimen 2*

The next morning, Specimen 2 stirred at an ungodly hour. I lay naked beside him, snuggled up against his lean torso, his wrists and ankles shackled to the bedposts as he slept. I decided to let him have one last natural night of sleep before I started the programming.

When he lurched awake, I sat up. He looked over at me and tried to talk, but he couldn't because he had a ball gag in his mouth. My head was swimming, the hour was so early, but it didn't take me long to focus. After all, this was the moment I had prepared for.

Early morning rays of the rising sun glinted through the barred casement windows, casting orange lines across his face. His eyes were wide in terror as he pulled at the restraints.

I calmly stood and went over to the nightstand. I opened it and retrieved one of my prepared hypodermic needles.

At first, I attempted to calm him by stroking his chest. He stopped jerking and lay fearfully under my touch, eyes wide, like an animal caught in a leg trap.

"Don't worry, everything is going to be absolutely perfect," I whispered to him.

He shook his head "no" and his muffled attempts at screaming only served to create some saliva dripping from the sides of the gag. I wiped away his drool with the bedsheet.

"You're so very lucky to be one of the chosen few," I assured him. "You'll see."

The needle went into his arm steadily and soon the serum worked its way through his system so that he could relax.

As I did with Specimen 1, I unshackled him and lifted him from the bed while I lined it with the sterilized plastic sheets and coverings. He was nearly half the size of Specimen 1 (in body mass, that is); it was like lifting a child. Specimen 2 likely didn't weigh more than 125 pounds. As with Specimen 1, I posed him in the rescue position.

After the bed was prepared, I lifted him back onto it. I didn't even need to get the stretcher, as he was easily within my bench-pressing limit. The shackles weren't necessary as he'd be out for a long time.

I checked the monitors in my lab and saw that Specimen 1 was still asleep. Any sane mortal would be, except athletes who had to jog at dawn. Never could understand how early-morning jogging was better than any-other-time-of-day jogging, but that's how this athlete rolls and I was ready for it. While he lay comatose, I hurried up to my own bedroom and took a hot, steamy shower. Once I was clean, dry and awake, I slipped on one of my lab coats and returned to his room.

The lab equipment was set up as before. Electrodes, monitors, oxygen. I worked quickly, making small incisions in his head, his torso, his genitals, where I inserted the tiny implants. When they were all in place, I cleaned him up and sterilized his wounds, changed the bedding, and all seemed to be in order.

I studied Specimen 2 with great fondness, staring at the droplets of blood that marked his initiation into my experiment. He breathed easily as the sedative coursed through his system. With a grin, I slipped the headphones around his ears. When sounds started pouring into his unconscious mind, I adjusted the frequencies on my handheld device to the calculations in my notebook. Athlete. No drinking. No smoking. No body fat. And so it goes.

He was so sweet, lying in bliss, his stigmata gleaming in the sunrise. He stayed like that for a few days.


*Specimen 1*

After the pub, haircut day, I took him to have a professional photo shoot the following day. That was a wonderful day. He was tamed with chastity underwear, a lightweight mesh and cotton that could fry his balls into bacon within four minutes, or kill him in five with a flick of the switch. He needed a portfolio for his book covers and various interviews. The photographer placed him into various poses for author photos—serious, playful, dog lover, coffee connoisseur, sexy, seductive, exploratory…

Specimen 1 was a natural, with his brooding good looks and lanky frame. He posed in front of a green screen and the photographer would add in various backgrounds to my specifications at a later date.


Today was that later date. I looked through the printed copies of the final set we had decided to use for press and media. My heart fluttered as I looked at the photos—his eyes were so blue, his chin strong and his firm body fit but not sculpted.

I was excited to go down to his suite and show him the pictures.

Over the course of the experiment, there was a bar set up for all of his cravings. There was alcohol of all kinds. Three kinds of scotch, four flavors of vodka, a beer fridge with a range of imported and domestic beer and wine. There was also a freezer full of ice and cartons of cigarettes. I bought several of those room purifiers so that he wouldn't be living in cigarette smoke, although he might as well be since he seemed to be a perpetual smoking machine.

I had to keep the air pure for my experiments. I determined how to set up a ventilation system that would send the smoke outside in a stronger manner than the bathroom fan could pull out.

So far, the ventilation appeared to be working well. There was barely the hint of cigarette smell in the air, and I could see one burning in the ashtray.

"Scott?" I looked around for him. I heard a bark from the side of the bed. "Scott?"

I walked over to the bed and there was Specimen 1, naked on all fours like a dog. He eagerly lapped at my feet and barked at me when I stood before him.

"Playing doggie today, are we?" I asked with my hands on my hips. He rubbed up against my leg, begging to be petted.

"Well, you'll like this. Your proofs came today." I waved the envelope at him but he did nothing but sit up.

"Enough, Scott, check it out, your proofs!" I tipped the envelope so that the multisized pictures would slide out. Specimen 1 tore the pictures out of my hands much as a dog would.

"Bad dog," I shouted as I gathered up the fallen pictures. Some had been destroyed, but there were still a few that were intact. It didn't really matter; they were just the proofs.

"Fine, you don't get to see your pictures. I'll choose what to send."

Scott circled around me on all fours with what appeared to be not a care in the world.

I sighed and fastened the envelope.

"Okay, go get dressed and we'll go do something."

I left the room quickly, but instead of getting dressed, Specimen 1 followed me down the hallway. I stopped and turned to him.

"Go get dressed," I spoke firmly. Specimen 1 sat on his haunches, tongue out, begging with his hands limp in front of his chest like paws.

"Okay, fine, you can watch me work."

He followed me up the stairs to my second-floor office. He wasn't to know about the basement office laboratory, nor about any of the other suites yet, but he already knew about the upstairs office and bedroom so it was better to go there.

I tossed the envelope onto my desk and slid into my chair at what I called Command Central. The security cameras were hidden behind the wall panels and I pulled up innocuous university papers on the computers.

Whatever I was working on, he would try to see it, would rustle through whatever papers and files I had stacked on the floor, knocking over my cups of pens and paper clips.

After a few hours of me trying to work with a human dog vacillating between demanding my attention, snuffling through my papers and sleep barking, I had to finally put him back down in his own office.

It was amusing and disturbing, all rolled into one. I wasn't too certain why he was suddenly in full-blown dog mode when we weren't playing a fetish game, but there it was. I poured over my calculations to see if I could bring his affections down a notch.

A part of me wonders if it's just an act. A scheme to lull me into complacency.

*Specimen 1*

The next day when I went into his room, he lunged at me angrily. This time instead of friendly dog, he was angry dog. He's a strong man and he took me off guard. His hands pressed around my throat, his legs wrapped around my chest trying to crush me.

"Why are you trying to kill me?" I screamed at him.

He barked and howled, his lips curled back as if he were showing drooling, dripping fangs when, in fact, he was just a pasty English guy having a temper tantrum.

In his attempts to grab my bracelet, he only made it worse for himself by knocking one of the charms that controlled some of his implants. He howled and screamed in pain as jolts of electricity shot through him. I took his painful moments as opportunities to kick him away from me and run across the room.

Specimen 1 twitched and yowled on the ground, his face grimaced in agony, turning so red I wondered if he'd have a stroke.

"Stop..." he screamed, at last uttering human words after two days of dogdom.

I found the charm that was hurting him and clicked the settings.

Specimen 1 lay panting on the floor.

"What the fuck?" he groaned. "What the fuck did you do to me?"

He rolled over onto his stomach and sobbed. I watched his shoulders shaking with his anguish. Part of me wanted to go over to him and comfort him, but the other part of me was waving red flags that this too was another ploy, another attempt to get me closer so he could try another attempt at escape.

When his sobs were reduced to whimpers, I crept out of the room and left him to his personal sorrows.

*Specimen 1*

The newest edition of a literary magazine arrived one day, the one that used the photos for the interview and PR patter to generate interest in the book he was working so hard on. The article was flattering and it would likely cheer up Specimen 1. I was happy to see him working on that very book when I entered his office. He took a sip of scotch before turning around to face me. His eyes were distant as I pulled him away from his fantasy world.

"Scott, look at this." I showed him the article. He took the magazine from my hands and read the piece. His expression turned to pleasure at first but by the time he finished the article, he was angry.

"Fine lot of good this does me," he said.

"What do you mean? It's a great article."

"I'm stuck here with you. I'll never get to enjoy my growing fame."

"Of course you will enjoy your fame."

"No I won't. You'll always have me all trussed up like a turkey, ready to destroy me with the click of a button."

"Oh, Scott, don't be silly. We will learn to trust each other, you'll see." I wrapped my arms around him. His pushed me away, standing up. He grabbed his scotch and drank again.

"Trust, huh? Is that all?" he scoffed. "Sure, I'll trust you. And you can trust me. Deal." He stuck out his hand. I took it and he squeezed it hard. "Look, Doctor, I don't know what you want from me but..." he leaned very close, "...I'll do my best to deliver."

I hadn't realized I was holding my breath and I almost sighed in relief, but now was not the time.

"Don't worry, Scott, things will change. You'll see."

As I made my notes, I remarked that it was good to see the real Specimen 1 back again. The subservient dog was just not his style.

*Specimen 1*

Weary, I sank into the warmth of my pillows with no other thoughts than to get as much sleep as I could in the least amount of time possible.

Once again, I woke in the night to find him standing over me. It wasn't as before—his stance was relaxed, even resigned. The dim light from the streetlights through the sheers gleamed in the reflective stare of his blue eyes. Strangely blue in the darkness, in fact. Like a scene out of *Sin City*. I wondered if the electromagnetic energies were affecting the pigment in his eyes. Regardless, the way he looked at me with such great sorrow piqued my interest.

I perched on my elbows, staring at him, wondering if my own eyes glowed with the same intensity. The curtains wafted as the air-conditioning kicked in. It finally seemed to be the correct moment to speak, but he turned and passed through the doorway into the hall. Soundless, his tall, naked body a shadow in the streetlights, he walked with a purpose away from me. I called after him as I swung my legs around on the bed, making the effort to rise, but he shut the door after him. The sound of his footsteps down the stairs faded away. I watched him make his way through the house and back to his room on the monitor on my cell phone. He didn't return and I didn't chase him.

I'm unclear about his motivation. Perhaps he still had longing for me. Perhaps he was formulating some kind of plan of his own. He was my intellectual equal in many ways. I'll have to be certain to keep an ample supply of his favorite liquors to embrace him in a daze thick enough to keep his curiosity at bay.

Of course, it could have all been a dream. After all, the man is supposed to be locked tightly in his chambers with no chance of escape. Somehow, he found a loophole.

*Journal*

Just as I suspected: After the incident the previous night, I devoted a few hours of time to reviewing some of the security footage from the cameras installed around the house. There he was. Specimen 1, trying the locked doors, prying with coat hangers and other objects when I wasn't around. He rummaged for keys in my offices and laboratories, opening and shutting drawers, crawling under desks, and knocking around for secret panels. He found lots of keys for various things, but whatever keys he was looking for were not within his grasp. He had no luck finding my many squirrel nests. But he was still curious.

His escape in the night had been a series of loopholes and missteps on my own account. I had forgotten to lock the tunnel from the basement to the first floor through the dining hall. Various skeleton keys, and I guess his own deft skill at breaking and entering, had enabled him to get from his room to my room. However, why didn't he just run away? If he'd gone so far, why didn't he just climb out one of the second-floor windows?

Perhaps he thought the windows were rigged. I did have scattered booby traps throughout the house, areas where touching a window or a door would result in an electrical shock. Of course, he was well aware of my bracelet and other devices, and perhaps had figured that if he tried to escape I'd just torture him further or even kill him.

So I had to top up the booze and add a formula to every bottle in the house to keep him less curious about everything.

Out of all my specimens, Specimen 1 has proven to be the most difficult to balance. Yes, I'm working with new technology, but his moody artistic temperament is more complicated than that of others I've worked on. His brain is bursting with intelligence and it's proving difficult to tame.

I will persevere to find the balance between adoration and obedience.

Specimen 2

While in my office transcribing notes, an image in one of the cameras caught my attention. It was Specimen 2, sitting up and looking around. He was tugging at the shackles, shaking his head as he tried to scream around the ball gag.

I removed my lab coat and checked myself in the mirror on the back of my office door. A blue T-shirt matched the blue contacts I wore that day. My favorite stretchy jeans clung to my ankles. My feet were bare.

I slipped on a pair of black leather, one-inch pumps and retreated to the room where Specimen 2 was wrestling with the chains.

"Hey, honey," I said as I approached him. Spit foamed around the ball gag. He stopped flopping around so that I could unbuckle it.

"What's going on here?" he cried out. "What the hell is all this? Fuck, I'm thirsty."

I went to the fridge on the far side of his bedroom suite and retrieved a small bottle of water. I also retrieved a couple of tea towels. In between his moans and groans, I held the bottle for him, which he slobbered on with his numb lips and tongue. His mewling like an animal was peculiar.

"You fell asleep, honey," I told him. He shook his head while continuing to drink. I used the other tea towel to wipe where he had urinated on himself. Pulling away the soiled sheets and blankets, I explained the situation to him.

"We were playing fetish games. You know how much you like the handcuffs. You fell asleep like that and so I left you."

"No...no..." he shook his head, "...there's more, I think. I dreamed..."

"Yes, you caught some sort of fever. A virus that's been going around. You likely caught it at one of your races. All those people spreading their germs everywhere. And incubation can take up to twenty-one days."

"No...no."

I pushed him back, rubbing his shoulders and arms, trying to ease the ache from the shackles that still contained him.

He began to moan again, a low, guttural sobbing chant. It was weird and I didn't like it one bit. The ball gag was returned to use and though he valiantly fought me, I managed to get him buckled in once more.

"You've been ill. In fact, I can show you the charts." On his dresser lay a few folders full of graphs and forms, charting the progress of his illness and the prognosis, combined with a quarantine period. There were clippings of newspaper warnings about conducting a quality quarantine so as not to create an epidemic. Of course, I had prepared the charts months before, much as I had similar sets of documents for all of my specimens. It was only a simple matter of adding date and sex, and most other information was the same.

"See, this shows the approximate time period when you may have contacted the virus. The strains of the virus are discussed in these papers here." I waved a stack of papers with photographs. Since he was chained and gagged, he had no choice but to look at the various papers I flashed at him. There was no point in letting him read them. This episode, too, would be another dream segment when next he woke.

After I took the soiled bedding into the laundry room and put it into the triple loader I had installed for just such tasks, I returned to the bedroom. From the closet, I took a long leather hammock-type contraption and hooked the four corners to his chains. I winched the chains very tight, which lifted his body above the bed. There was no way I would attempt to winch Specimen 1, as he was nearly 200 pounds and the weight wouldn't be good for the wood posters of the bed, although the posters would likely sustain him. However, for

Specimen 2, with the metal bedframe and his lithe body, it was a breeze to hoist him up.

I finished pulling away the soiled bedding from underneath him. I wiped down the plastic sheet with an environmentally friendly lemon-salt mixture and rinsed it well. Once I wiped it dry, it was quite the task pulling fitted clean sheets underneath his flailing, angry body. Even though he was suspended slightly above me, he tried his damnedest to hit or rock against me. Poor little triathlete. The chains were impossibly tight and he could barely wiggle two inches in any direction.

Instead of knocking him out, I wanted to observe his strength when awake. Although a small man, he was very strong. I was gauging if the metal bed and the studs through the walls and into the beams would be enough to hold him when I wasn't near to observe him.

To keep him calm or perhaps to agitate him, I spoke in a low, reassuring voice while I set about my duties.

"You'll have to stay here for a while. You're quite ill and since I'm a doctor, I've arranged to care for you while you're under quarantine. In fact, you will have to be here some time so your apartment is being packed up for storage, except for your racing bikes, some clothes and a few other things you might need."

There was much commotion, with the chains rattling and the hammock swinging. I had finished with the bedding and set to work lowering him back down. Since he was so agitated, I had to sedate him to calm him down.

*Journal*

It took one week to program Specimen 2.

Once he was ready to function on his own again, it was time for him to meet Specimen 1.

If Specimen 1 had suspected that there might be someone else, he had never said anything.

"Scott, I have something to share with you," I told him one day as I went into his office. Scott spun around in his chair.

"I hate it when you say that. It usually means that something isn't going to go well for me," he said.

"On the contrary, you may find this interesting, if not delightful. I've added another male to our lifestyle. Perhaps you can even be friends."

"Huh?" Specimen 1 was clearly confused. "I'm not gay…"

"Oh, you don't have to fuck him or anything, unless you want to. But I wanted you to know that I've been spending less time with you as I've been preparing a new Sp…friend for us. I want you to meet him later on today."

"Not that I have a choice."

I laughed. "No, not that you have a choice."

"So, what's up?"

"We'll all have dinner together and then we can get to know each other. I'll see you at six in the dining room."

"Yes, ma'am," Specimen 1 said as he turned back to his work.

"And your novel?"

"Working on rewrites. Will be asking you to send it soon."

"Excellent…"

*Journal*

Dinner was...interesting.

Specimen 1 was seated at six in the dining hall, which was up on the main floor of the house and only used once in a while. I had a tunnel from the back stairs entrance into the dining hall. The doors were all locked, no windows—there's no way for the boys to escape.

The dining room was one of my favorite rooms. The mahogany table was long enough to seat sixteen on either side, with the hostess on the end. There was a lengthy side bar and several tall locked cabinets with china and serving dishes. Every item in the room was heavy and reinforced with locks, as it could be so easy for a specimen to get uppity and start to trash the place. I'd been down that road before and didn't relish traveling it again.

I led in Specimen 2, who had decided to be feisty, which meant that I had to put a shock collar on him to make him behave. Of course, after the first shock, he became quiet and didn't bother attempting escape or tackling me. I had dressed him in a yellow T-shirt and jeans. His brown hair was a bit longish since he'd not had a cut since he'd come here.

Specimen 1 looked very handsome, wearing a casual blue shirt that brought out the vibrancy of his eyes, his blond hair slightly gelled into the little spikes that I liked. He probably wore faded jeans, though I couldn't see under the table.

"Scott, here's our new companion. This is Peter, our resident triathlete," I said holding Specimen 2 by a leash attached to his collar.

Specimen 1, born and bred with English manners, stood up and approached Specimen 2 with his hand out.

"Welcome, Peter."

Specimen 2 turned away from Specimen 1's outstretched hand. "What the hell is this?" Specimen 2 yelled. "Now I have to service you too? What the hell is going on?"

I tugged at Specimen 2's leash. "Calm down or you'll get another shock."

"I'm like you, old chap," said Specimen 1. "I'm here because Miriam took a liking to me, much as I guess she has to you. I didn't know you were here until a couple of hours ago."

"I've been here much too long," Specimen 2 said angrily. "I want to go home."

Specimen 1 laughed and pulled out a chair for Specimen 2.

"You might as well sit down and enjoy the meal. What Miriam wants, Miriam gets, and if she wants to add you to her collection, then that's how it rolls."

Specimen 2 stared at Specimen 1 and then looked at me and at the chair. He sat down.

Specimen 1 pulled a chair out for me and I sat down.

"Very well, gentlemen," I said. "I see Scott has decanted the wine and poured us each a glass. Shall I toast my fine young gentlemen?"

We all raised our glasses. Specimen 2 looked completely confused and agitated, but he had no choice about anything at this point. He seemed resigned to his fate for a few minutes and clicked the glasses.

"I'm so thrilled to have such talent with me at this time," I said. "Two very talented men with fabulous careers." There was silence in the room as the men waited for me to continue.

"Scott is a best-selling novelist," I said.

"I'm not on the best sellers list, although I'm close," he corrected.

"It won't be long, my lovely," I said as I turned towards Specimen 2. "And Peter is a triathlete who competes in the Iron Man and such."

They stared at each other and silence fell across the room. Specimen 1 drained his wine and poured himself another.

"Read any good books lately?" he said to Specimen 2, half in jest.

"Not much of a reader," Specimen 2 said, staring at his nearly full glass of wine. "I'm also not much of a drinker."

"Sorry to hear that," Specimen 1 said. He turned towards me. "So, lovely Doctor, what's on the menu tonight? I'm famished."

I grinned and stood up. "You boys should be delighted with tonight's dinner. I ordered in from one of my favorite restaurants."

I walked over to the side bar where half a dozen large silver trays with covers were displayed.

One by one, I carried the trays over while Specimen 1 uncovered them. Heavenly smells wafted through the room. There was roasted chicken, beef medallions with gravy, mashed potatoes, green beans, two kinds of salads and cheesecake for dessert.

Specimen 1 and I dug in; we both were foodies and loved our red meat and potatoes. Specimen 2 stared with dismay at the offerings.

"Not hungry? You've been on solid foods for a while now…"

"If I'm under quarantine, why is HE here?" Specimen 2 said.

Specimen 1 laughed.

"Quarantine? What web did we weave for this little fly?" Specimen 1 mocked.

"Scott has an immunity to your virus," I explained.

"Peter, I'm sure you're not ill at all. This doctor of ours, this mad scientist, is keeping us prisoner for some reason that I've yet to really understand. But then, who understands why anyone would keep people locked in their basement?"

"You're a prisoner?" Peter asked.

"Oh, most certainly. And believe me, Peter, don't get any fancy ideas about escape. She has your balls in a vise, likely literally. One touch of any button, she'll get you. There's no escape, so just enjoy." Specimen 1 downed another glass of wine and poured more. I had finished my wine and he filled my glass again.

"Miriam?" Peter asked. "We're prisoners?"

"I wouldn't call it that. You two fit the profile of a highly secretive and important experiment I'm conducting for the government. I can't talk about it yet, but you should be honored that you're here at all."

Specimen 1 laughed.

"She's so full of shit. Don't listen to her lies. However, it's not really so bad. At least it hasn't been for me. I can drink all I desire, and all I really do is sit at my computer writing all day anyways, so life hasn't changed too drastically for me. And when she's feeling really generous, she takes me out to parties and such. Kind of like her pet."

"Why, Miriam?" Specimen 2 asked. "Why are you doing this?"

"You ask a lot of questions," I said. "Enjoy your dinner. Don't you like what I have here for you?"

Specimen 2 looked at the food.

"Yes and no. I mean, I'm supposed to be in training. I can't be eating things like mashed potatoes."

"I'll eat yours for you," Specimen 1 said, scooping a second helping onto his own plate. He slathered more butter and gravy onto the mound.

"You seriously should eat. She doesn't go all out like this every night."

Specimen 2 reached for one of the green, leafy salads. He spooned most of it onto his plate.

"You can have chicken, I'm sure," I said, lifting a piece of chicken from the serving tray and putting it onto his plate.

"Yes, I can have lots of meat if I know I'm going to be working out."

"I'll make sure you both get exercise tonight, don't worry," I said seductively. Specimen 2 stared at me. Specimen 1 nodded.

"I'm sure she has all kinds of things in store for us," Specimen 1 said.

"I do," I said.

"Listen, once you prove you can behave, she'll give you more freedom." Specimen 1 winked across the table.

"He speaks the truth. You need to train for your meets and I want you to train for your meets, so it's up to you how soon you want to get back on track."

Specimen 1 laughed.

"Clever with your words, Doctor." He clinked my glass.

Specimen 2's face continued to grow longer with horror. "I'm really stuck here…"

"It's a new phase to your life. You'll enjoy it. Behave and she'll give you a good time," Specimen 1 said. "Any pleasure you desire, it's yours."

"Why?" he asked me. A simple question.

"Why what?" I continued to eat my dinner as we chatted across the long table.

"Why did you pick me to spoil like this?" he asked.

"Why indeed…" I said.

"I mean, you met me at a sex club. Now you want to pamper me just to fuck you? I don't get the catch," Specimen 2 said.

"The catch is you never leave," Specimen 1 said.

"That isn't really true, is it? I mean, I figure, you pick me up at the club a couple of times, you like my big cock and endurance. You're not the first to sing such praises of me. Rock stars aren't the only ones with fans."

"She's a horny old lady," Specimen 1 said, raising his glass to me. He drank the remainder in one gulp and reached for the bottle again. After he poured another glass, offering some to me and Specimen 2, which we refused, he cut into his chicken.

"What Dr. Miriam wants, she gets. You'll see. You're likely picked because you have a big cock and stamina. She's studying you."

Specimen 2 looked from Specimen 1 to me.

"Are you?" he asked. "Studying us?"

I laughed. "Scientists always study. Writers always write. Athletes always athlete…" I let the silly word hang. "Whether I'm aware of it or not, I'm constantly studying human behavior and the brain's electrical impulses. It's just what I do."

"But you're not really studying us, like in a fancy paper with a grant kind of experiment, are you? I mean, don't we have to give consent and all of that?" Specimen 2 said.

"You, my darling, contracted a very interesting strain of influenza, necrotizing fasciitis borreliosis, and had to be quarantined here, remember?"

Specimen 1 snorted and poured himself another glass of wine.

"How long is this so-called quarantine?" Specimen 2 asked.

I paused and took a sip of my wine.

"Until the tests indicate that the disease has cleared from your system and you're no longer able to infect anyone."

"What about you? What about him?" Specimen 2 asked.

"We've been vaccinated," I said. Specimen 1 shrugged.

"I could have been. Who knows what the hell she's done to me."

Specimen 2 grew pale. I began to play with my charm bracelet, staring intently at Specimen 1.

"What do you mean by that?" Specimen 2 asked. Specimen 1 stared back at me, my fingers on the bracelet, and frowned.

"Nothing...nothing... Come now, let's eat before this delicious meal shrivels up on us."

The rest of the meal was spent in silence. But by the time I brought out some cognac, we were all very relaxed.

"Let's go down to Scott's room," I said standing up, holding my glass in one hand and the cognac bottle in the other.

"Sure, why not!" Scott said, grabbing another bottle of wine from the side bar as he led us down the back passage and through the secret hallway where one of the locked doors led to his section of the basement.

We watched TV for a little while, with me in the middle of the men. I had tripped specific switches in the panel of one of each of their charms at several points during the awkward dinner. By now, as predicted, they both had noticeable swells in their jeans. I rubbed each one of my hands on each one of their thighs. I turned to Specimen 2 and kissed him full on the lips.

"See? This isn't so bad, is it?" I asked him softly as I pulled away. One of his hands cupped my breast. I turned my face towards Specimen 1 and kissed him. He held my face in his hands, pressing his lips against mine in tender, slow brushes. My own body swelled with excitement, my own implants tingling as they yearned to merge with each of the Specimen's. I imagined the blood of three bodies entwining, the energy circuits surging and rushing, stopping and starting with hesitation, and undulating with urgency.

Before long, our clothes were off. I lay back, enjoying the twin sensations of my favorite men pleasuring me. My mind raced with every wet lick of their tongues—how vibrant their energy was, how it danced pleasurably with my own. They took turns eating my pussy, each one teasing me to a new height so that I'd come in the other one's mouth. My loss of control in the ecstasy was nearly complete but I was always acutely aware of where my bracelet was at all times, my fingers always near the "panic button".

When I'd had enough of cunnilingus, I pushed them from me.

"Your turn, boys," I said, standing in front of them. They both turned to stare at me, their eyes wide with lust, their wills weakened with passion. I knew I looked powerful, my eyes flashing in the dim light of the TV screen, my large, high breasts and narrow waist, my long, firm thighs, all looked magnificent in this light. I caught a glimpse of myself in one of the mirrors and could see that this session was just what the doctor ordered.

"Sit down, both of you," I commanded. They both sat on the couch. I went over to one of Specimen 1's cabinets and brought out lube, towels, wet wipes, Kleenex and three bottles of water. Always practical, I placed them on the coffee table that was pushed back from the front of the couch.

I approached Specimen 1 with a stern look. I lowered myself to my knees and took what I could of him into my mouth. He groaned with the sudden pleasure. My free hand found Specimen 2's cock and I stroked him while giving head to Specimen 1.

After giving back to the boys for a while, my jaw was growing numb so I climbed onto Specimen 1's lap and sat facing away from him. I played with him for a while, teasing him with my pussy while I reached for the lube. I poured some into my hand and then slid it along his cock. He moaned and I lowered my ass onto him. The deliberate slowness of my lowering down onto him resulted in great pleasure for him. It was difficult to gauge whether he'd actually ever been that hard inside my actual pussy since the two orifices were very different on me.

The pleasure of him inside of me began to grow, the initial rough rawness of penetration replaced by a soothing massage. My pussy trembled with anticipation.

"Come to me," I said to Specimen 2, holding out my arms. Specimen 1 didn't miss a stroke as Specimen 2 slid home. We rocked together, a weird and crazy trio. They worked in a great rhythm, anticipating my needs, riding me on every wave of pleasure. At all times, I kept sight of my bracelet, no matter how high ecstasy took me. If I lost control for one minute, they could overpower me.

We were a sea of slick sweat and juices by the time we were done. By the end of it all, we had wound up on the floor in a maze of pillows, panting and laughing. The towels were already well used, so I stood up to go to the bathroom. I left the men exhausted, Specimen 2 already asleep. I found new towels and gave one to Specimen 1. With another I wiped Specimen 2.

"Wake up, sleepyhead. Time to go to your own room."

"Oh. I just want to sleep here. Please…" he begged.

"No, I'm sorry, it's off to bed with you." I picked him up and slung him over my shoulder. Specimen 1 looked at me as if he'd seen a freak show.

"Christ, you're strong," he said with awe.

"Don't you forget it," I said. "Good night."

I carried Specimen 2 out into the hall. I locked the door from the outside. Still naked, I put Specimen 2 to bed and back into his shackles. He didn't even resist, he was so exhausted. I had to chuckle. He had great stamina until he came. Then he crumpled like a popped balloon. The hour was very late for him, for all of us.

I retreated to my own room and spent a fabulous rest of the night reliving the glorious threesome. This was a lifestyle I could definitely embrace.

I hope Specimen 3 works out just as nicely.


*Specimen 2*

Specimen 2 listened to Specimen 1's advice. He stopped fighting me on every little thing and soon was permitted to wander around his apartment by himself.

We had dinner every night, with it culminating in Specimen 1's TV-library room, since he had one and Specimen 2 didn't.

After about three days, I began to let him and Specimen 1 comingle. I kept the hallway between their suites unlocked so they could visit with each other. The doors to the outside world were still kept bolted and electronically charged so that they couldn't escape. I made the effort to have evening meals in the dining hall to keep our little unit cohesive.

The day before, a special delivery had been made to the house. Several huge boxes had arrived and I was excited to share the contents with Specimen 2.

I took him upstairs to the main floor so that he could help me carry the boxes down. He wore the dog collar in case he tried to escape or overpower me in any way.

"I have some surprises for you," I told him.

"What is it?" he asked.

"First, your bikes have arrived. These three boxes are your bikes, equipment from your apartment and some clothes and other things that I thought you might like to have here with you."

"Really?" He rushed over to the boxes and ripped open the first one. The yellow gleam of one of his beloved bike frames was revealed. "Oh my God, I thought I'd never see you again."

He tore open the rest of the box and pulled the cardboard and foam packaging away from the bike.

"You can keep it in your room. We'll put hooks on your wall, just like you had in your apartment."

He hugged the bike as if it were a long-lost puppy that had finally made its way back to him. "You have no idea how much I love this bike."

"I'm beginning to see," I said.

We unpacked the crates from his apartment first. When that was completed, I showed him the other boxes. Very large boxes.

"These are for you too. Some new state-of-the-art equipment for your training."

He tore open the boxes to find more training equipment. An elliptical, an exercise bike, a medicine ball, weights, a bench and much more.

It took several hours to unpack, haul the stuff down to his room and then set it up. I had considered asking Specimen 1 to help us, but he wasn't really the athletic type. This was more of a bonding job between me and Specimen 2. I hadn't had my workout that day so it suited me fine to be hauling things down the stairs. I did have secret elevators at the back of the house, but I didn't want Specimen 2 to know about them.

Once his equipment was set up, he actually looked the happiest I'd seen him since his arrival so many weeks ago.

"You will need to begin training right away," I told him. "You have some meets coming up, if I'm not mistaken."

"I don't even know what day it is," he said.

"Don't worry about dates. Just start your training."

"How will I train on the bike?"

"You have that new bike over there," I said pointing at the state-of-the-art exercise bike with every gadget imaginable that we'd just assembled.

"But I need to ride outside, get my bike working properly. Surely you're not keeping me under house arrest."

"You can earn the privilege of exercising in the real world. Step by step, my dear."

"Whatever that means. When's this quarantine over?"

I ignored his petulance.

"I have my own work to attend to," I said as I turned to leave.

"Enjoy your new gym, my dear."

I left his room and locked it, hearing him screaming obscenities as I left him there.

## Specimen 3

I had quite a workout helping Specimen 2, so I took a long, hot shower. The steam relaxed my tired muscles and the scent of musky, gingery shower gel filled the room. My hair was short so I let it get wet. Currently, it was red again.

In my bedroom, I tried to decide what to wear. Looking at the clock, it seemed that a bathrobe was in order. I wrapped myself in a black velvet bathrobe and sat down at my vanity table while running a comb through my damp hair. My flesh was pale so I added a bit of eyeliner and some dark shadow to liven up my eyes and a dab of red lipstick so I didn't look like a corpse.

Given the late hour, there would be no going back to the lab. I checked the boys in the security cameras. Specimen 1 was at his computer, clicking away, stopping now and again to light a cigarette or to sip his scotch. Specimen 2 was riding the exercise bike while watching a DVD of some triathlon, his jaw set with determination. I hoped he wouldn't overdo it. He'd been dormant for weeks and may not have his usual strength.

There was an email from Specimen 3 in my inbox I had seen on my BlackBerry earlier and preferred to respond to with the ease of a computer keyboard at my leisure.

When I opened the email, I saw that she was online that very minute, so I clicked over to chat with her.

We both had our webcams on and it was a pleasant surprise to see her face once more. Her green eyes were vibrant, even through the webcam technology, her lips freshly painted, her skin reflecting the lamps that shone on her in her bedroom. Behind her was her bed, a simple queen with a girly flowery bedspread and very ordinary wooden headboard. There appeared to be a boxy dresser in the background and not much else in the tiny room.

"When are you coming to see me?" I asked her through Skype.

"I don't know," she said. She smiled coyly at me and tossed her chemically straightened, dyed-blonde hair. The heart shape of her face was still breathtaking. I grinned back, touching my neck with a long, slender finger.

"You need to come soon. I want to wine and dine you," I said. "Don't you want to be pampered?"

She giggled and waved her hand.

"Who doesn't want to be pampered? By the way, I want to thank you again for the MP3 earpiece. I love it." She held it up to the camera. "I wear it all the time."

"I'm glad you're enjoying it. Here, I found another song for you." I clicked the Messenger icon and sent her two more MP3s that I had specifically programmed for her. I hoped she truly was listening to them but, even now, just in chatting with me, I was transmitting subliminal coding to her unconscious mind through the computers. It was a technique I'd not yet perfected as, of course, studies and theories about brain-computer communication and restructuring of pathways vary vastly between scientist, computer technology and psychiatry. Can it be done? We all agree it can. But to what extent, how long does it take, how long does it last?

What was happening to her now was related to my voice patterning. Imprinting my voice with sensations of want and desire, of need and pleasure. Her brain is learning that when she hears my voice, pleasant sensations will occur in her body.

"Hey, this looks cool." I could see her hooking her MP3 player to the computer portal, or at least she was reaching as if that was what she was doing. She played the song loud enough that I could hear it.

Her beauty glowed from the screen in a translucent gleam. It was magnificent to view.

She was perfection, even in an imperfect telecast. Between the flickering phosphors there lay the beauty of the universe, emanating one pixel at a time, a charisma few others contain.

"It's one of my favorite songs right now," I said. "It reminds me of you."

"You're so sweet." She giggled.

"So when is it you're coming to see me?" I asked again more earnestly.

"It's just that I'm looking for work. I have to be here, ready, for when a job comes."

"Why don't you look for work here? That's what brought you here last time, wasn't it?"

She laughed.

"Sort of."

I nodded.

"So that man was the one who brought you here? The one you were with that night. Was it an acting gig?"

"Of sorts."

"Ah…" I nodded. "So what would it cost for you to come and see me for a week? Airfare and all."

"I-I… Well, ten grand," she said, suddenly more businesslike than I'd ever seen her. For a moment, it disturbed me, this sudden harshness from this fair creature, yet the lightning that sparked her into life quickened my desire. This fetching cherub beckoned to me, my only payment mere money to buy the time to bask in her splendor. In staring at her smooth chocolate cheeks and bright, almond-shaped eyes, I would pledge more than mere money. A soul could be but a mere pittance of an exchange if only to share breath with an angel.

"Ten grand, eh?" I said. I leaned back in my chair, my bathrobe sliding open under my fingertips until my breasts were nearly completely exposed. I ran my hands lightly across my chest.

"Ten grand…" I murmured. Her lip had a bit of a sneer before her face softened into angelic beauty once more. She sat back in her chair so that I could see the round mounds of her breasts heaved up over the purple lace of her underwired bra.

"So all I have to do is give you ten grand and you'll come to see me?" I asked. I tapped my lips with my long, painted nails.

"Yes." She smiled as she traced the swells of her cleavage with the MP3 player that she'd unplugged from the computer.

"Interac transfer okay?"

She frowned and sat up.

"Oh no, it has to be cash. I'll come there on my own devices and you pay me cash when I arrive. No paper trails."

I laughed. Oh, she thought she was one clever cookie.

"A one-way ticket, right?" I said, never losing my cool as my fingers danced around my chest, pulling at the sides of the velvet robe.

"Of course. I'm not paying for a round trip."

I squeezed my breasts together.

"You won't have to pay for a thing, my dear," I said.

She rubbed her breasts for a moment, but it was clear her attention was on other chat windows as well. I watched her eyes stare at first one area of the screen and then another, suddenly her fingers were clicking the keys, but no messages arrived for me. After watching her for a moment, I grew impatient.

"Book your ticket and email me the details," I said. She jolted at the sound of my voice, as if she'd forgotten me already. She looked into the camera and winked.

"I will, honey. I have a few details to attend to before I can leave town." She made a valiant effort to keep her eyes from wavering to the other chat windows but in the end the chat window on the lower right-hand side of the screen won the wager.

"Do what you have to," I said as she typed something to someone, somewhere.

"I will, honey." She waved with one hand, while the other one typed.

"Good night." I clicked her away.

My excitement was boundless. How magnificent it was going to be to add the beauty to my growing family.

*Journal*

My observations are aligned with most of the theories I'd speculated about going into this experiment. The fine tuning took much longer than anticipated although this time there was the time, space and resources to indulge in fine tuning, instead of aborting the experiment. Now that the men are regulated we've begun to establish a normal life and routines.

Each specimen has his own zone and each has everything he needs or desires. To feed each man's ego, his cave is filled with citations of his accomplishments and photographs of winning awards and trophies. Both of my specimens excel in their fields, with their fields being very different from each other, so there is no need to worry about battling egos. I don't doubt that Specimen 1 considers Specimen 2 beneath him intellectually, while Specimen 2 understands that Specimen 1 has no desire to run marathons or lift weights.

Each specimen has a daily dose of "music" either piped into his apartment or through his headset should he listen to one of his music devices. This daily dose of music is key to their programming.

Each specimen has total freedom to explore the subject of his pursuit. Specimen 1 writes and drinks and smokes all day. He enjoys reading and watching TV.

Specimen 2 works out and receives a special diet six times a day. He watches TV a lot. Usually sports.

The hallway that connects their rooms is left open. They will sometimes visit each other during the course of a day, but it's not usual.

Routine works well for everyone. Around ten, when my schedule allows, the three of us watch TV together on one of their couches. I'm always the instigator. I'll kiss one and then the other. I'll touch them both, rubbing my hands along their inner thighs while we watch TV and neck. Before long, hands are touching flesh, clothes are torn away and we become a triad of writhing, sweaty flesh. The boys both pleasure me, taking turns, sometimes both at once. Their eagerness to please ignites my desire, their seasoned touches fan the flames of ecstasy.

Though I enjoy their pleasure greedily, I always take care of theirs as well. Each specimen has to be treated fairly and equally. A man can't feel threatened or inadequate, or the triad won't work. His needs must be observed and then satisfied. A satisfied man can focus on his work and excel in his field, which in turn creates a healthy self-esteem and healthy sex drive.

We often fall asleep on the couch, limbs tangled with each other, our lust exhausted at last.

At some point, I always manage to pry myself away and return to my own room.

The balance is working very well.

It will be interesting to see what happens when Specimen 3 arrives.


*Specimen 2*

Specimen 2 was running on the elliptical, his breath panting out in spurts, his face frozen in tense concentration as he stared at the runners on the big-screen TV in front of him, TV announcer yelling excitedly about the race. Somehow I didn't believe his eyes were seeing the runners at all.

He didn't notice me watching him at first, but when he did, he muted the TV. As he slowed down his pace, he reached for his towel and wiped his sweat-drenched face.

"What is it?" he asked. He seemed vaguely annoyed by my presence.

"I think it's time you went outside," I said.

"Really?" he asked.

"Yes. You can take your bike out for two hours. You must return here within two hours. If you don't, then I will push this charm on my bracelet and you will blow up."

He stared at my charm bracelet, eyeing the golden dancing bear dangling down from dozens of other charms.

"You're ridiculous," he said as he hopped off the elliptical. "You wouldn't blow me up."

"Why not? It's the only way to keep you from telling."

"Huh."

"Not the only way. One of many ways. See this one?" I fingered a tiny brass monkey holding a tin cup. I squeezed it slightly. Specimen 2's eyes grew large and he grabbed his balls.

"What the hell?"

"That's low. You don't want to feel high. One wrong word from your lips and your balls are toast. Literally."

"How?" He shoved his hands down the front of his gym shorts and felt around his genitals. For a brief moment, I worried that he had found something but there was nothing.

"I don't feel anything," he admitted. "Well, except for the pain you just inflicted on me."

"There's nothing to feel and nothing to worry about. Go on your bike ride and return within two hours and you won't have to worry about a thing."

He returned in one hour and forty-five minutes. He had followed instructions. More details are in the other journal, such as his vital signs. He was loaded down with more spy gear than a James Bond character. There was no room for any slippage. One word, gesture, eye contact or anything else could spell ruin for me.

He cycled along city streets until he got to High Park, where he spent most of the time weaving along the trails. He didn't stop anywhere, except to briefly rest at one point. He didn't speak with anyone at all.

He passed the test and so he was allowed out every day for two hours.

*Journal*

I'm the first to admit that I'm not as diligent at checking the surveillance footage as I could be. There is so much of it and I'd need to be three people to watch all that potential evidence, let alone earn a living and conduct my experiments.

I do watch them live, catching glimpses of them throughout the day, spot-checking what they're discussing from time to time, but as time goes on, I get back to real-life focus.

My observations at this point seem to be that Specimen 1 has toned down his key searches and other prying behaviors considerably. Likely since his deadline is nearly here he needs to focus on completing that final round of edits. Once that book is completed, he has to dive immediately into the next one, plus deal with the press I've set up for him.

Specimen 2 never was curious. Once the drugs left Specimen 2's system, any memory of his previous life seemed to have gone along with it. He never really talked about his past nor seemed to want to see family or friends. He never spoke about his job. It was like he woke up at my house, newly born, *tabula rasa*, and all he knows is his athletic events. I wonder if in my desire to not screw up, like I did with Specimen 1, I overcompensated in some area—memory, curiosity?

Specimen 1 may be playing me if he noticed the boost in his booze. The compound should be tasteless but he has a refined palate. I scan the tapes when possible but I know I'm missing events I should really know about. But what can I do? I have no assistant to watch twenty-four hours a day tapes that may or may not prove there's something I need to know.

*Specimen 3*

The day had come at last when she arrived on my doorstep, bright California sunshine on a dark, wintery, stormy day. The weather had suddenly turned two days before. As typical in this unstable climate, one day Specimen 2 was out riding his bike in the sunshine, and then the next day the temperature dropped fifteen degrees and a sudden hail storm hit. The wind and sleet made leaving the house a nightmare for anyone. It seemed odd to me that she somehow showed up on this day, when I was certain that the airport had been shut down for hours.

"Come in quickly," I. She wore a toque, a hooded parka and heavy boots. I found it odd that a California girl would come equipped with a parka and boots. There is some more background checking to be done with her. I was so enamored of her and so preoccupied with the boys that something has escaped me from her files.

She stomped her feet on the outdoor mat before coming into the house. She quickly removed her coat and boots, and I whisked them off to dry in the parlor bathroom, hanging them on one of the hooks I'd installed over the heater. It was a great coat-warming spot. I used it all the time for myself. When I returned, she was fluffing her hair and staring around the hallway. She wore a jersey-knit minidress and black stockings. Chunky turquoise jewelry she wore around her neck and wrists spoke to me more of Ontario aboriginal art than anything Santa Fe. Her countenance seemed off-kilter, something in her vibration that wasn't quite correct.

"How was your flight?" I asked her as I led her through to the kitchen. My kitchen was a stainless-steel wonderment and could be used to prepare food for one or for fifty. When I first purchased the home, it had been set up as a party kitchen, with two ovens and all kinds of features, such as two fridges plus a wine cooler and a beer tap. I was going to have them all removed but as I got deeper into my experiments, I realized how convenient having choices could be, especially when I was entertaining.

I poured water into the kettle and plugged it in.

"I... Okay." She smiled. "I could really use an espresso. Do you have that?"

"Of course," I said as I pulled out my small one-cup espresso maker. I quickly ground a fresh batch of beans and in a few minutes she was sipping her espresso and still not telling me about how she magically appeared on my doorstep.

"The weather's not usually this bad this early in the season," I told her.

"Sure it is. It's downright schizophrenic."

"I suppose it is. Shall we go to the living room?"

She placed her cup on the kitchen counter.

"We haven't even said hello to each other properly yet," she said with a pout. With a start, I remembered that I'd better get focused on the reason she was here and worry about the details later.

I hugged her, holding her tightly.

"I'm so excited you could make it. We're going to have so much fun."

She kissed me warmly on the mouth and then a glow of excitement flushed her cheeks.

"This kitchen is so huge. You must have some amazing kitchen parties."

"Yes, I most certainly do." I backed her against a counter and kissed her again. She hugged me close, her hands cupping my ass through my jeans.

She was much shorter without the tall heels that she had worn, but her shapely legs more than made up for it.

She broke the kiss.

"Don't forget the money," she said, suddenly businesslike.

"Of course," I said. I left her and went upstairs to my office where I pulled two thousand dollars out of my filing cabinet. I shoved it into an envelope.

I returned to the kitchen where I thrust it into her hands.

"There will be much more, don't you worry," I promised her. She peeked inside the envelope and giggled at the hundred-dollar bills.

We kissed hungrily, eager for real-life consummation that we'd never had. I pushed her towards the living room and onto the couch.

My hands cupped her breasts and I kissed them, eager to touch and taste her. It wasn't hard to liberate her of her minidress and me from my jeans.

"Sit there," I instructed her and she sat on one of my plush velvet chairs. Her beauty filled the room, her soft, supple flesh, her flashing green eyes, her lovely soft smells enticing me to madness. I spread her legs and pressed my face into her soft, perfumed pussy. My tongue explored her, gently at first, and then my licks grew more urgent as my excitement grew. I slid my fingers into her, sucking on her clit while fucking her with my hand. My beauty squirmed and wriggled under my touch.

"Ooo, that's so wonderful." She sighed. "More…"

Under her guidance, my tongue danced and my fingers stroked her until she was shivering and quivering towards climax. I pushed her G-spot and as she came, she flooded me with her slick, sweet juices. I eagerly caught her ejaculate, licking harder and faster, bringing her to orgasm after orgasm.

Finally, I pulled away from her with a grin. She laughed and stroked my hair.

"You were magnificent." She moaned. "I think I'm going to enjoy my time here."

*Specimen 3*

Specimen 3 is fussy. I realize it takes great energy to be a goddess, but her constant demands for beauty products and fancy clothes is new to me. I comply by taking her on shopping trips. She's a princess, true and true.

She tastes so delicious, and she likes to taste me too.

After she had been with me for a week, I set about programming her. She is light and easy and seemed to be ready to integrate after about six days.

*Journal*

I introduced Specimen 3 to the men. At first, they kept looking at me as if this was some sort of test they were going to fail. They both knew by now not to say or do anything to alarm Specimen 3.

We sat in the dining hall. Specimen 1 lifted his glass.

"Welcome to our family," Specimen 1 said.

"Thank you," Specimen 3 said, warily looking at Specimens 1 and 2. "I think I'm going to like it here."

After dinner, we all went to Specimen 1's room to watch TV and spent the night rolling around with each other. The men took turns fucking her at my insistence. She enjoyed every inch of their large, enthusiastic cocks, begging for more.

We must have spent hours fucking and sucking each other. Everyone got along magnificently. I was very pleased with the combination of beauty, brains and brawn.

*Specimen 1*

We had what I thought was a whirlwind afternoon. There was a press conference held at the university where reporters of all kinds came to interview Scott Gravenhurst about his newest book. The place was crawling with reporters, Specimen 1 constantly posing for cameras from the minute we arrived at the campus until we hailed a taxi just to escape from them.

There had been a question-and-answer period and about four hours where several different reporters in various mediums interviewed him.

There was so much fuss about this budding young star and the world was holding its breath in anticipation of the novel he had delivered. This was a straight-to-print literary genre book, one of the rare combinations that either sailed high above every other one or sank like a rock in the quicksand of elitism.

Specimen 1 was in his glory, charisma kicked into high gear as he performed with the charm and vitality that had originally attracted me. He occasionally glanced over to me, always a look of panic until he found me and his gazed locked with mine. Then he would seemingly relax and fall back into the rhythm of promoting.

Once we were home behind closed doors, things changed. I had thought that we could have a nice late-night drink to celebrate the parties and interviews, but instead he grew sullen.

"I don't want to speak with you right now," he said as he turned his back to me. He began to unbutton his shirt. "I wish you would leave, please. I need some time to myself."

I turned and left him. As I twisted the double-keyed locks, and fastened the bolt to his section of the basement, I mused on how frustrated he must be to not be able to go out carousing with his writer friends and perhaps scooping up a budding young writer he could show the ropes to. Instead, he was here, trapped in a woman's fantasy, a pawn to be played with so her quest for ultimate knowledge, ultimate pleasure, ultimate happiness would be satiated.

*Journal*

It has been three months since Specimen 3 has been added to the family. She was even easier to program than Specimen 2. I believe it's related to the complications of the speed of rerouting existing patterns into new ones. Everyone can have his own theory about the length of time it takes to form or unform a habit, lifestyle, religious ideology and so on. Each brain is so much the same and yet so completely different in the slightest of nuances. Why is it that drinking two bottles of beer can affect each person's perception in so many different ways? Some people might be drunk, some sober, some may have an allergic reaction or just fall asleep. The same with the serum and electromagnetic combinations.

I wonder if the electromagnetic forces flowing through all of our bodies constantly will have any long-term effects.

I've not noticed any real symptoms except that I'm constantly horny and will likely wear those boys out before they hit their forties. But the buzzing in my crotch mates the buzzing in their minds and if I ever turn it off, they will be gone. Wherever the implants go, they will follow.

The boys are good providers. Specimen 1 sells well and Specimen 2 receives loads of prize money.

I earn money from my essays and books, and even give lectures now and again on neurological transmissions through electromagnetic fields with regard to human behavior patterns.

We want for nothing in our strange little arrangement.

However, the addition of Specimen 3 is still not going well. Her beauty is a full-time job. Jars of lotions, pots of creams, hours of lying under lamps or heated fabrics, soaking in tubs, standing in showers. Every week, she wanted to go to the hairdresser for a different weave and a mani-pedi. I, of course, enjoy changing my hair frequently as well, so I didn't really mind going together to the beauty parlor. I'm not quite so attentive to my hands and toes, though, and don't have the patience to sit through weekly mani-pedis. I'd do work on my tablet while she was pampered, and of course, spy on my men.

It didn't matter that we had our weekly beauty visits; she still had to care for all her nails at home as well. It was a constant entertainment for her, all her self-pampering.

You'd think she was a movie star and, indeed, she likely aspired to be just that.

I sent out her portfolio for more modeling work; however, her reputation as lazy and demanding meant that despite her magnificent beauty and charisma, people didn't want to work with her. She'd blown up her bridges at the young age of twenty-two.

With more prying and probing, it was also an underground secret that she was a hooker, an escort, a cokehead, and, therefore, no major studio would ever cast her in a movie. Since I'm not in the arts, I don't understand why it matters if she's a hooker or not. Last I heard, everyone from Marilyn to Madonna slept their way to the top—why not my beauty?

It didn't matter.

She always was a star when the four of us went to the clubs.

However, her grating requests, her constant demands for more, more, more was not the docile, relaxed goddess that I had hoped for. And the fact that she cost more than both the boys put together, with zero income, didn't help her case that much.

There is always a payoff. I didn't want to up her doses too much, for becoming a dog or anything else wouldn't be useful with her. I could snap her like a twig with my own fingers should I want, my strength was no match for her frail beauty.

Still, I wanted beauty, I had my beauty.

Yet, something doesn't feel quite right.

*Journal*

When I returned home from the university, I had an odd feeling in my bones. Scrolling through the cameras wasn't giving me any information, as all the specimens had their TVs running in darkened rooms. After removing my coat and putting down my purse and briefcase, I went down to the basement and began the task of unlocking all the bolts. My gut was clenched. My heart pounded and my anxiety was completely unfounded. Why I had the nervous stomach was startling to me but I knew there was a reason.

Before I finished unlocking the doors, I went into my lab to grab several hypodermic needles that I kept prepared in the fridge. I filled my pockets with them, my only weapons. I didn't know what I was going to find behind those locked doors but it wasn't going to be pleasant.

There was hope that my paranoia was unfounded, but years of this game indicated to me that my instincts were going to unfortunately prove to be correct.

The last lock unbolted, I walked quickly down the hallway, one hand in my lab coat, ready for anyone sneaking around corners and such. The mirrors in the corners of the hallways were intact—so no surprises around any corners.

My gut determined that I check Specimen 3's room first.

My damnable gut had been accurate and turned sour as I stood there with my mouth hanging open like some dumb idiot in a horror movie.

There they were, engaged in erotic activity without me. Specimen 3 was sitting on Specimen 2 while Specimen 1 slammed into her with such delirium that they didn't hear me come in. They moaned and rocked, a perpetual motion machine. It was hypnotically enticing in a way, watching three beautiful people. However, their flaunting of the rules was not beautiful at all. This is not part of the rules. This is not how it goes. They are all to crave only me and not ever dare to try one sexual escapade without me around.

And yet, there they were and I wonder now how many other times have they all had fun behind my back?

"What is this?" I said, my voice low as I fought to keep my anger.

"Oh." Specimen 1 saw me first and pulled out. Specimen 3 quickly disengaged from Specimen 2 and they stared guiltily at me.

"Just having a bit of fun," Specimen 1 said, his erection beginning to soften. "Figured you wouldn't mind…being out and all."

It felt like I'd been punched in the stomach. Speechless, I gaped at them like a fish out of water. Every cliché in the world overwhelmed me, but that was not me. I was not a cliché. I was more than that. I was more than some authority figure to be mocked behind my back. Love and respect would not let them cheat on me. The equation was overwhelming as I comprehended the programming failure. It took me a moment to regain my composure.

"You have all broken the rules. There will be consequences."

I didn't say any more and backed out of the room. They didn't move or speak until I shut the door.

It took a hot, steamy shower to calm my nerves. My head was spinning; I was literally quivering with rage. I wrapped myself in a large terry-cloth robe and climbed into my large, warm bed. Clicking the remote, I opened up the windows of sixteen of the security cameras and started the analysis time-stamped when I left the house.

When I was out giving a lecture, I had left them to their own devices. All of their doors were open. They were free to roam at will. The live footage I was able to sneak peeks at during my event seemed innocuous. But the way they acted upon my return gave me the chills.

Specimen 3 leaned out her door to call for Specimen 1. She said she was having a problem with the TV reception and needed help. He entered the room and they flirted with each other for a bit. She pointed to the remote and he fiddled with it for a while until it was adjusted to her liking. She excused herself to the washroom. He stared at the TV for a moment but kept glancing towards the bathroom. He went into the bathroom.

I had a tiny camera installed in the bathroom, but the picture wasn't clear because of the distortion of the lens and the steam from showers. There were glimpses of them kissing passionately. Then, all too clear, between the mist smudges, he was taking her on the floor. She cried out with pleasure, her face, that beautiful face, contorted as he pleased her.

A pang hit me in my abdomen. My passion for them both was crushed. It wasn't as if I'd never watched them before; it was the joy they had at disobeying my orders.

The lack of control sickened me.

They had quite a time in that bathroom. I fast forwarded and their session lasted at least an hour, with a steamy shower.

As tears welled up in my eyes, I reached over to click off the remote when I see her donning a little pair of short-shorts and a halter top. I watch for about four minutes and she returns, laughing, with Specimen 2 in tow. He doesn't talk much and they fall into her bed in an embrace. She must know there's a camera there, Specimen 1 certainly had spotted it, but perhaps Specimen 3 didn't believe it or notice it.

The betrayal hurts me more than I expected it to. It was not an unexpected action and something I should have been more emotionally prepared for. Humans have been breaking the rules since the first day they existed. Historically, has there ever been healthy respect for authority or love or commitment? True human nature always finds a loophole. However, the entire experience caught me off guard and my dominance needed to be reestablished with all three of them.

*Journal*

Beauty…what was beautiful about her really? Genetics? Was she beautiful inside and out?

No, she was a filthy liar and her star continued to dim in my mind. Her betrayal and lies consumed me. Each day, another little slice in my heart as something else proved that she was less perfection than most of the people I worked with every day.

Women cheating women. She took my men and used them as her own. She didn't respect my boundaries as her lover. The programming hadn't reached deep enough for any of them. What made them so enticing, their oozing sexuality, also made temptations too easy and the reprograming of so many pathways to worship only me was too delicate. It had never been done, that I was aware of, unless there were other people like me conducting such experiments in their basements. It's not impossible, but unlikely.

I've set up more powerful infrared spycams in every area of the house. Not so much for catching them at play. It matters not if they cheat once or a thousand times. After one time, it's done as far as I'm concerned. It just becomes a Springer show after that. Careful observation of behavioral patterns is needed and physical reactions to the experiments must be explored in more detail than ever before.


I'm adjusting the formula and am going to try a chemical neurological compound that may trigger a specific set of synapses to respond to the new audio subliminal stimulus.

I will see just how effective each phase is as I adjust the formulas.


*Specimen 3*

I enter her room where she's been tied to the bed for two days. The smell of the place was disgusting and I pulled my germ mask over my face. Earlier I'd sprinkled drops of lavender into the mask so that I wouldn't be subjected to Specimen 3's wretchedness.

She was quiet, watching me with fearful eyes.

"I hope you've had some time to reflect on choices you've made." I stood by her side of the bed. She lay naked on plastic sheets, smeared with her own feces and urine. A tube snaked down from the headboard and into her shoulder where there was an intravenous tube to keep her hydrated and vital. Plastic sheets lined the floor and walls and most of the furniture. Her eyes were wide, she was sweaty and making crying noises through her ball gag.

"You can't, you just can't run around fucking my boyfriends behind my back. There are rules. In any sexual arrangement there are rules, spoken or unspoken, and they are to be followed." I paced around her, staring into her eyes. My own were brown today, dark and daring. She tried to squirm, the chains rattling against the wooden frame of her white princess canopy bed.

"Your pretty white room is getting pretty filthy with all this mess you're making," I said. I turned and walked away. I gave her a moment to believe that I was gone. I waited a few minutes. I rolled a metal table into the room. The disappointment on her face when she saw that I had returned was priceless. Her fear began again, a panicked struggle, as if she hadn't already tried every form of escape over the past two days. The trolley clinked as I rolled it near the bed.

I went over to where she lay frozen with fear, her eyes carefully watching every detail of what I was doing as I pulled the tubing needle free from her shoulder. She winced a bit as the needle left her flesh and only a few droplets of blood emerged until I pressed my vinyl-clad finger over it for a minute.

The bleeding stopped so I tidied up the equipment by closing the secret compartment cupboard where the IV unit was hidden in the headboard. The needle and tubing were disposed of in the hazardous-waste barrel in the corner of her room. Items could be dispensed into the barrel but not removed. I only brought the barrel in when I knew there would be big jobs such as ones involving plastic sheets and feces.

I wore gloves and the mask and a long-sleeved vinyl apron over my lab coat. I uncinched the chains and they rumbled loose until she could move her arms freely. I uncuffed her and rubbed her wrists. She didn't have the energy to claw at me. I unshackled her legs. She slid around in her own filth, trying to get the feeling back.

I removed the sheet covering the trolley. The shelves held cleaning supplies, towels, bedding, plastic, disposable wipes, sprays and more. In the side panel was a leather riding crop and a leather flogger.

"Stand up," I commanded. I knew it would be hard for her. Plastic sheets slid between her feet as she faltered. Her eyes were lost, great foamy loops of spit dripped down from the ball gag and her chin. "You made quite a mess here. You'd better clean it up."

She pointed at her own body where she was filthy, but I ignored her gestures.

"Clean this place up. You need to wipe down the plastic before you roll it up. Use the disposable towelettes and put them in the big barrel."

She stood there. I went to raise my flogger but I didn't really want to as she was covered in shit and it would be a waste of three thousand dollars worth of braided leather.

"Fine. Go take a shower, but, remember, you drip on the way, that's more mess for you."

She was clever as she wiped the worst of the sludge from her legs and feet and put the waste into the disposable barrel.

When she was satisfied the bottom of her feet were clean enough, she carefully made her way to the bathroom. I watched her take a long, steamy shower. It was nice to smell her soapy freshness again instead of that hideous shit smell. I knocked on the shower stall door.

"Excuse me," I said as she looked out. I reached up to her head and unbuckled her ball gag. It was a bit tough, as it was wet, but at last I was able to do it. "Rinse this off in the shower and give it to me."

She turned back to the shower and soaped up the ball then rinsed it clean.

She stuck her hand back out of the shower with the gag and then dropped it into my hands.

"Thank you."

She began to hum, the beating of the water washing away her filth likely a soothing baptism. Specimen 3 began to sing; long and lovely notes from one of the songs I'd sent her reverberated around the bathroom. My ache for her began once more as her siren song lulled me. I knew she was calling me but I resisted. This would be a battle of wills and the princess *will* succumb to the queen.

Her singing gave me goose bumps, my flesh stung and shuddered with each note her perfectly pitched voice slid along. Her harmonics were magnificent, a delicate tremor that reminded me of the ultimate vulnerability we all have. She was hypnotizing me with my own music. On the bracelet, there were charms for my own implants. For the first time in a long time, I was going to have to use them to keep her from seducing me.

I found the magician with his little magic wand and rubbed it. A subtle shift in my electrical current was barely detected. I don't think it would be noticeable to someone who didn't know she had an implant. I tweaked another charm, a ringmaster. There was no sensation at all from that one.

The singing stopped and she stepped out of the shower. She turned to me and looked rather smug. I frowned.

"You need to go clean up your mess. Now." I snapped the flogger at the backs of her thighs while she reached for a towel from the drying rack. She stood quickly as the leather strips slapped her legs.

"Holy shit," she said, rubbing her legs.

"Go," I said, striking her naked ass before she could get her towel.

"Yes, I'm going. I promise. Really." She wrapped the towel around herself and went into her bedroom. She stared at the mess. She put the towel back in the bathroom.

"Might as well clean naked. Less mess that way, I guess." She ventured back into the plastic, slime-coated hell and spent about three hours cleaning it up to my satisfaction. Once every last bit of rot had been cared for, I allowed her another shower. While she was in there that time, I removed the waste barrel to a garbage room in the back of the basement. There were stairs behind a wood-paneled wall that led from the basement up into one of the backyard sheds.

I lounged on one of the couches in the newly cleaned room while I listened to her fidget around the bathroom. I watched her antics on my watch. She appeared resigned to her fate, ready to succumb to my whims.

When at last she appeared, she had blow-dried her hair and had perfect makeup on her face.

"I wanted to please you, Doctor," she said with a slight bow.

"We'll see how you please me. Get on the bed."

She climbed up onto the bed, looking at me expectantly.

"Back into the cuffs," I said firmly.

"Already? Really?" She pouted.

I reached for the remote control on her dresser. "Yes, now, please, or you know what will happen."

She sighed and stared silently up at the ceiling while I fastened the cuffs around her arms and legs. I cinched everything tight so that she was splayed out. Not too tight, so that circulation could flow but there would be no escape.

As I took the ball gag from my pocket she started screaming.

"I don't want it. I'll be good. I promise. Please don't make me wear that."

Luckily, a head-shaking, screaming princess is easily coaxed into submission. The gag is popped back into her mouth and I buckle the head strap. I adjusted the shackles so that she was closer to the right-hand side of the bed and down near the end of it. Her legs were spread very wide.

I rolled over a lighted mirror and magnifier that I had taken from my laboratory. I adjusted it so that the arm swung out enough that I had a full view of her genitals.

Satisfied that there was enough light, I went back down the multilocked doorways and hallways to my laboratory. There was a kit I had prepared earlier in the day that I needed to get. I also brought some anesthetic and a rolling stool and extra plastic sheets.

I returned to her and set the stool down. I sat on top of it and opened up my kit. The needle and thread were already sterilized and ready. There were several backups and a variety of sizes.

"Since you don't seem to understand how to keep your legs closed, I'm going to have to do it for you," I said firmly. I pinched both sides of her *labia majora* together, taking care to push her clitoris way down so as not to nick it. The needle took quite a bit of pressure to push through the thick flesh, but at last I figured out the best angle. I pulled black thread through her flesh. She moaned and struggled, or at least her muscles clenched in the urge to struggle, but her actual movement was nil.

In and out, the needle tugged and punctured, thread pulled, fresh holes oozed dripping blood. By the time I was finished, my handiwork was neat and precise. I had left small openings for her period and for urinating. There was no way to get even a lady's baby finger up into her through the stitches.

I sprayed alcohol along the wounds, the chains clattering against the wall as she twitched.

"We have to make sure that you don't get infected," I said to her as she moaned. "Who knows what germs might be lurking around? All those men. All those stolen moments."

I let the alcohol drip along her legs and onto the plastic sheets. She was shaking, the pain was so intense. Yet there was nothing she could do.

"Next time you want to steal someone's man, you think about this little scenario we're having right now."

I hovered over her and grinned.

"You know, it's a good thing I brought you here. Who knows how many other women you've hurt by fucking their men."

Tears were rolling down her face as she blinked rapidly at me. I laughed and walked over to the dresser where the riding crop lay. I picked it up, swinging it in the air.

"I've done a good thing, taking you from the streets. You may have fancied yourself a model but you were really no more than a whore. An escort between gigs. You've probably made more money as a whore than you ever did with an honest living."

I slapped her legs with the crop.

"How many of those men were married? How many of them spent the family grocery money on whores like you?"

I struck her breasts with the crop, slashing back and forth.

"You need to be taught better manners. I let you run wild in your time here. Now I see that I was mistaken. I wasn't firm enough with you. The worm has turned, my dear. Your rule in my kingdom is now over. You will learn your place. The dirt beneath my shoe is too good for you."

I left her with those thoughts and, no doubt, an insane amount of pain. We'll see how soon she considers touching my property again.

*Specimen 1*

I didn't punish him as long as the others. I knew his participation was for a different reason. I also was well aware that he had to spend each available minute chasing his muse. So he was only shackled for nighttime and portions of the day as his punishment.

*Specimen 2*

I kept him in shackles for two full days. Once the time had passed, I set him free. After I allowed him to shower and clean up his filth, I made him go into the gym portion of his room.

"Lean over your bike," I commanded him. "I want to see your ass."

He bent over the bike obligingly. I approached him and then began to spank him.

"Hey," he called out.

I spanked him again. "What is my name?"

"Doctor Miriam Frederick," he said.

"What is it that you will never do again?"

"Cheat on you."

"No. You. Won't." I punctuated each word with a slap and then stood back. My hand stung but it was a good feeling.

When Specimen 2 was satisfied that the session was over, he stood up.

"What is it you won't do?" I asked him.

"Cheat on you," he said.

"Thank you."

I turned from him and left the room. I didn't return to see him for another two days but I pushed basic meals through his door flap.


*Journal*

It was time to have some fun. The boys needed to adore me once more under more familiar and entertaining conditions. I changed the coordinates on Specimens 1 and 2 and me so that we would have a lusty evening connected to each other but open to explorations.

I took the boys to the fetish club, leather chaps and collars on both with chain-link leashes attached to soft suede straps in my hand. I danced with them and flogged them soundly on the spank benches. I didn't make them wear chastity belts and decided that if anything happened then I would just have to disappear.

There are boxes and suitcases in place should any of my experiments ever escape and are able to relay their stories before I can either deprogram them or destroy them. I'm ready for my own escape into obscurity, a selection of false IDs and documents at my fingertips, open-ended plane-ticket vouchers to many parts of the world. One must always prepare for the worst, as they say.

However, tonight, the specimens made me proud in the dungeon at the fetish club. Specimen 1 was handcuffed to a St. Andrew's Cross, back to me, and I flogged him with great joy. A crowd had formed to watch this performance art of two handsome men in dog collars and chaps crawling around to the whims of a masked dominatrix in head-to-toe leather. The outfit was incredibly hot to wear but the admiring glances at my tall, lean body made the sweat worthwhile. I'd never be able to wear that outfit again after the amount of sweat that was absorbed into that hide.

But in the moment, the catsuit and the leather boots were stealing the show.

One of the benefits of age was the years of practice I'd had in wielding a flogger. Even if I hadn't used one in months, the minute the weighted handle was snug in my palm and my fingers clasped around it, I knew exactly how to swing.

Since we were in public and since this was supposed to be a night of erotica, I didn't flog either one of them in a punishing manner. Indeed, my whole demeanor had been one of showmanship, playing to the spectators, some so painfully shy that one could drown in the sweat of their repressed anticipation of perhaps tasting the flogger themselves someday.

My slaves stayed by my side, flanking me by crawling on all fours through the crowded bar, curling up by my feet while I waited for my drink at the bar. Even crawling through the sludge of the filthy, flooded bathroom, they stayed on all fours.

The last time I went to the bathroom, after I finished my business—which took one hell of a time in that tiny stall in the catsuit, but I was successful—I returned to them sitting at attention on their haunches by the sinks.

"Stand up," I told them.

They did.

"Okay, we're done here. Why don't you both freshen up a bit and we'll go to the next place."

"Where?" Specimen 1 asked.

"Silence."

They washed their faces and naked chests. Soon they were clean of the filth of the club. We bought perfumes and toiletries from the bathroom lady, and before long, the boys were fresh enough for anywhere.

At the coat check, they slipped off their chaps and dressed in shirts and leather pants. They both had leather boots and jackets.

I hailed a cab and we went to the sex club.

It was very busy and soon we were on the dance floor with our drinks, sourcing out couples to take into the private rooms. Specimen 1 danced near a short, blonde, buxom girl who was with a tall, tanned man. I danced near them and Specimen 2. Before long, another couple was migrating into our circle of gyrations and dirty dancing. Our lusty energy infested the dance floor as everyone humped to the techno music in the flashing lights.

After a few numbers, I took the boys by their hands.

"Join us in the back," I called out to the other couples. "Please, come play."

They followed us through the change rooms where we were assigned lockers and keys by a pretty, naked brunette who couldn't have been more than eighteen.

The night was still rather young so there were still a few rooms left, as well as the open areas. Mattresses were everywhere and the pack of us lay down naked on the giant bed, kissing and touching, all nervous locker-talk babble now lost in kissing and sucking.

I crawled from man to man to woman to man and every combination there was. My specimens were well within my sight at all times, there was only one door and I always was certain that, no matter how crazy the position or how many men were shoving their cocks into me at once, I was between the door and my specimens.

My libido kept me craving more and more. I was insatiable, riding wave after wave of orgasm, greedily climbing on cock after cock, even pushing the other women away. I realized much of the groaning and grunting was coming from me.

It was in that moment, another moment of exquisite orgasm, that I understood that I was becoming lost inside my own experience. I was being reduced to my primal nature instead of being the observant doctor.

It was a tricky tightrope, for the end result of the experiment really did only benefit me. The essence of the specimens would live on forever, but despite the illusion of love I was feeling for my specimens, it was but an illusion. A chemical reaction to sex and closeness and habit. Nothing more and nothing less.

*Journal*

I purposely left the three of them alone for the first time since I caught them. Upon my return I reviewed the recordings and everyone did as they should. Specimen 1 drank whiskey and wrote and surfed the Net. Specimen 2 went for long bike rides and runs and from the bugs I have in both his shorts and his bike, I know where he goes, where he stops, I can hear conversations. He has seen no one of interest in his wanderings. His discipline applies to the rules I've set for him, as well as his own goals. Specimen 3 stayed in her room, watching TV and pampering herself. They didn't even seem to communicate at all in my absence.

*Journal*

For one week, I punished Specimen 3 with her sewn-up chastity.

On the eighth day, I brought her a glass of wine. She wore a knee-length ruby-red satin T-shirt dress and she had braided tiny, long, multicolored strips of ribbon into her hair as she lounged on the couch, feet hanging over the side, her pretty toes painted red. Her eyes glimmered with sorrow, combined with a catlike expression of serenity. It was the cat part that always kept me on guard, knowing that despite my superior identifiable intelligence, the cat was secretive, calculating, cunning and cold. She could strike at me with one deft claw for no reason at all.

One hand held the crystal goblet of red wine, my other hand firmly grasped the braided handle of the flogger.

"What do you want from me now, Doctor?" she asked, gingerly sitting up.

"I want you to enjoy this glass of wine," I said as I handed it to her. She took it, eyeing it suspiciously. "What new torture do you have for me?"

I laughed as I sat down beside her.

"I have no tortures for you. All of these actions have been the result of your betrayal. How do I know you won't betray me again?"

"I've learned my lesson, Doctor, believe me," she said with an attitude.

"Stand up," I commanded as I jumped to my feet.

"Why? I just got this glass of wine."

"You may not drink it yet. Put it down," I ordered.

She glared at me with all of the hate in the world. Her hate didn't bother me. She should hate me, it was healthy and it was normal.

Specimen 3 put the wineglass down on the coffee table and stepped out into the wider area of the living room.

"Pull up your nightgown." She pulled it up so that I could see the result of my handiwork. Some of the threads had frayed, there were spots were the flesh had torn and bled and scabbed, other spots with the beginning ooze of infection.

"Still intact, I see," I said, studying the thread. She nodded.

"Yes, Doctor. I'm never going to break your rules again. I promise. Never."

"Next time will be worse."

She didn't say anything as she dropped her nightie and turned away.

"Go to the dresser," I said. She walked over to the dresser. "Bend over and hike up your skirt."

She bent over and I flogged her several times. She was silent, though she stared at me the whole time with hatred narrowing her eyes.

"Line your bed with the plastic, please," I said, pointing to a stack of plastic sheets I'd brought into her room earlier that day.

"Oh, not again. What are you going to do to me this time?" she half sobbed. "I'm so tired. I want to go home."

I stopped in my tracks and stared at her. Where was beauty? Where was her fragile innocence? Had I killed my creature in my quest for control? Had I plucked the wings from the fairy queen?

This was not beauty. Strong, confident, self-aggrandizing beauty.

I held up my wrist, looking at the dangling charms. I fondled one of a cherub and clicked his wings several times. She jerked a bit as the electrodes readjusted. She stood taller, a grin graced her lips, even her skin seemed to glow.

She undulated in front of me, stretching and swaying, her silky gown clinging to her nipples.

"Mmm, Doctor, are you going to play with me?" she asked in the soft voice that had first lured me to her.

I touched her face and brushed her lip with my finger.

"The game has but begun," I said. "There is more."

I snapped the flogger in the air and nodded towards the larger area of her suite where she did her workouts and yoga. There were floor-to-ceiling mirrors on nearly every wall, so the beauty could see herself quite well in her gym.

I pressed a button in one of the wall panels and a set of shackles dropped from little doors in the ceiling. They were bolted to steel beams that ran the length of the basement ceiling. I had installed when I built the suites. These were same type beams that I used for hoisting and shackling in the men's apartments.

Once she was shackled at the wrists and ankles, standing in the gym, chained to the ceiling and walls, I flogged her again. This time when I beat her, she'd catcall me, feisty and spitting, angry that I punished her for doing something that she'd done a million times in front of me—so what's the difference?

What *is* the difference? Some people would speculate and, quite rightly, that there's no difference in sharing in front or behind someone's back. If consent is given, is it a blanket consent? Where is the line?

Others say there's a time and place. There's a game and there's reality. There's permission and there's lying.

My rage flew beneath the flogging and her taunting turned to quiet grunts of pain. At last, I had finished, and she was streaked with whip marks from shoulders to calves on all sides. If I were a cannibal, I'd consider her halfway to tenderized.

She had tears in her eyes as I approached her. I decided that I didn't want to hear her weeping so I retrieved her ball gag from the drawer.

"No, don't put that on me. I'll stop, I will," she begged. I quietly and patiently got her head locked into the device, despite her strong-willed actions attempting to dodge me.

I had to go to my lab to retrieve my tiny scissors, tweezers, wet wipes and some little bags. When I returned to her, she was nearly limp, her head tilted down.

It didn't matter to me. The less squirming, the better for this part. I kneeled down before her and began the tedious task of snipping the threads that had tied her shut. Carefully, I pulled at the threads with the tweezers, coaxing them out. As the blood flowed, I wiped it away with the wet wipes.

She moaned, awake again with the agony of my pinching and pulling, the sting of antiseptic, the ache of her arms in the air while this was going on.

At last the task was done. I wiped down the area one last time. It wasn't pretty in the normal sense, but the pattern that the scars would ultimately form was unique.

I took my garbage and my tools back to the lab and made several notes in the other journal.

When I returned, she was still dripping blood in spots and had lapsed back into a semidream state.

I unshackled her hands first and dropped her gently to the floor. I unshackled her feet and rubbed her extremities to be certain the blood was flowing properly again. I removed the ball gag, wiping the drool from her face.

As I lifted her into my arms, she woke a bit and stared up at me.

"I love you, Doctor," she whispered and fell back into unconsciousness. I lay her on the plastic sheets and stared at her for several moments. Beautiful creature once more, naked, crisscrossed with rising welts, blood seeping from the holes in her labia. She had the face of an angel.

*Journal*

The three of them were watching TV innocently, as they used to do before things got out of hand. I entered the room.

"We should do something, all four of us," I announced. Specimen 3 yawned and filed her nails.

"Not today, I hope. I'm tired."

"Tired from what? All you do is lie around and primp," Specimen 1 chided. "Hell, at least the two of us work for a living, as limited as we are."

"Oh right, Mr. Best-Selling Novelist, how I must offend you with my ignorant presence," she said.

"Well, really, what do you do? You've not even had a modeling gig since you landed here," Specimen 1 sneered.

"Getting fat anyways," Specimen 2 taunted. "Why don't you put away that chocolate for once?"

"Hey, guys, stop it. I wanted to take us all out." I stood before them, staring at them with hope. However, the way they looked back at me, with varying degrees of disdain and laziness, my enthusiasm waned. The idea of getting ready to go out, keeping track of three people—all of it suddenly exhausted me. I turned away from them and ignored any more comments.

I left the room and the basement. Instead, I went to my own bedroom, grabbed a bottle of red wine and my pot box and watched a pile of movies: *Gone with the Wind*, *Diamonds Are a Girl's Best Friend* and *Planet of the Apes*.

I didn't even check the monitors once.

*Journal*

It was during a lecture that I was giving at the university that it dawned on me.

I didn't have to live like this. As much as I'd created this new situation that was causing me enormous stress and agitation, instead of the pleasure and harmony I'd envisioned, I could uncreate it. How silly we can be when we're too close to our own lives.

I'd aborted many experiments over the years. One more or one less wasn't going to make a difference.

I'm not ending this experiment—I'm going to enhance it, strengthen it, define what qualities are truly vital for living in that suspended moment of great and distinct pleasure.

*Journal*

As with any experiment, good or bad, there has to be a time for the observations to draw to a close. The next phase of the experiment would have to begin.

Specimen 3's beauty was wearing thin with her narcissistic demands. Her lure of the boys to spite me was downright blatant at times. She was particularly enamored of Specimen 2 with his endless stamina and would selfishly work him harder than anyone, since she knew that she could.

I certainly had no issues with Specimen 1 and his pleasuring skills. I just enjoyed having both of them, at my leisure, in the sequence I desired, not having to wait for Specimen 3 to stop hoarding Specimen 2, especially when she knew he was mine.

Specimen 3 had healed quickly after her ordeal and she seemed to enjoy herself as much as she ever had.

As Specimen 1 was licking my clit, I looked over at her hands and knees on the bed, Specimen 2 pounding her from behind. She leaned down towards me and kissed me.

The brush of her lips against mine didn't thrill me anymore, the glowing light in her green eyes was vacant and sinister, her long, manicured claws were ready to scratch at any given moment. She looked back at Specimen 2 and oohed at him. I glared at her until Specimen 1 turned my face towards his and kissed me.

"At least pretend you care that I'm fucking you," he said. "I'd rather be watching TV myself."

I clutched his ass with my fingers, pulling him deep inside of me while kissing him, our tongues dancing as new enthusiasm overwhelmed both of us. As Specimen 1 took me to ecstasy, I looked over at Specimen 3 squeaking with every thrust made into her by Specimen 2.

The goddess was falling from her pedestal, my pedestal, bit by bit, crack by crack, until she would be nothing but shattered dust.

*Specimen 3*

I sit in my office, trying to write some notes but my glance keeps going back to Specimen 3 on the monitor. Her days are endlessly tedious. I can't stand to watch them; I don't know how she can stand to live them.

I stare at the surveillance cameras. She's been picking at her face for over an hour. I don't know what she sees there or what she's picking at. Over and over. Then she starts with the creams and lotions. Playing with hairstyles. Trying on outfits and matching the shoes to them. It makes me want to scream. But that's what a beauty does, it would seem. I have actually kept logs of how many times she changes her outfits and other such nonsense, in case it comes in handy another time when I write a paper on the princesses and their behavior.

She files her long claws. I know what's next. She'll sit on her couch with a million cotton balls and little bottles of different colors. She'll stare at the TV screen and during commercials will paint her finger- and toenails wild combinations of colors.

There's a roll of fat that hangs over the waist of her short-shorts. The sight of it distresses me. She needs to work out more, but it's so exhausting making these three specimens go through their rituals every single day.

I click over to Specimen 1. He's sitting at his desk, smoking, with his glass of scotch on the rocks, and staring at his computer screen. I zoom in on what he's looking at. It's an online article about his book and an interview with him, flanked by one of the photos he posed for that day so long ago. He sat staring at the screen for a very long time, and with the exception of drinking and smoking, he was as still as a statue. Of course, I'd put the article there, as I did everything I'd find of interest on the real Internet and then route into the false-shell environment I had created for the specimens.

It wasn't the first time he'd seen the article either. I'd shown it to him myself the day it came out.

Whatever emotions were going through him, he didn't show them. He just stared, drank and smoked.

Specimen 2 was manic. I barely watched him for a minute. Specimen 3 lay around like a lazy lion; Specimen 2 was like having a hyperactive squirrel scampering around, except for when he was watching TV. Then he just sat and ate, hypnotized by flickering images.

I clicked back over to Specimen 1. At last he closed the window with the article and resumed his writing.

Specimen 3 was still painting her nails.

The article I was preparing was to be presented at a conference in a few months. I was hoping to have more complete results by this point but something had happened along the way. The sexual nirvana I thought I would be experiencing still eluded me.

There could be no more pondering, no more attempts to glean which route was the auspicious one to take. I could consult tarot cards, I could consult textbooks—it mattered not. The experiment had too many factors and the complications compounded one another.

I watched Specimen 3 painting her nails. I took my own bottle of polish from my desk drawer and touched up a couple of nicks as I pondered my options.

*Specimen 3*

Denial of the transformation has continued. I'm having a difficult time and have tried in vain to coerce and tease other types of behavior from her, ones that involve altruism and empathy, but she is a shell, a hollow puppet that reflects and refracts whomever she's with. Flirtations have their place. Cruelty and betrayal are no longer tolerated from her.

I'm not sure why I thought I could lure a goddess to earth and expect her to stay a goddess. It was time to release her to where she truly belonged. She was disrupting the harmony of the perfect life that I had spent years mastering. Codes and formulas, psychoanalysis, rhythm and tonality, degree upon degree, study upon study, all fit together in a complex matrix to stimulate the brain to crave specific things.

I didn't have it quite right with any of them—have I not just spent the last few pages lamenting that very idea? However, her blatant betrayal was the worst. It stung me right in the heart. Was it because she was a woman? Was it because she was all that I was not and never would or could be?

Yet I despised her too. I despised how she let life happen to her, even as an escort. She only needed to pout and preen, and she had a home and anything else she desired. Women like me had to work for a living. We had to be as good as, or even smarter than, men. And those of us who are beautiful have it worst of all. It's amazing how societal norms and gender-specific expectations can color a lifestyle, a career, a marriage.

Specimen 3 graced many covers of magazines, she was a red-carpet wannabe, a celebrity-climbing succubus. Like so many before her and after her, she was a product of our ridiculous society.

The beauty was manufactured and replicated, easy to spin and design. The beauty I had seen that first night, that lusty shine which had spoken of goddesses and forbidden moments, was long gone. Crashed from the heavens, dropped from the world.


*Journal*

The boys have started to hang out together more at the end of the day. In fact, I noticed over the past week they are slipping into a whole different routine. Specimen 2 hasn't been waking up early. Specimen 1 hasn't been writing as long. Before a few days have passed, they sleep in, play video games all afternoon, have dinner with me, and then we all get together.

But they are soft. They don't have their spark of excitement.

Was this a rebellion or is there something in the formulas I need to adjust yet again?

It's midafternoon. The sun gleams in from the skylight. I'm in one of the attic rooms, where the sun beams down. This room has monitors for my cameras, the door is hidden by a bookcase on the other side. Sometimes I like to sit in the sun with my laptop. It's like a change of scenery. The sun is warm on my face and it's soothing.

With a few clicks, the monitors are on, split screens displaying twelve camera views at a time. There are hundreds of cameras throughout the house, I keep adding more as I think of different angles I might want to see.

The men are playing video games. They lie on the couch, screaming at the TV, writhing with the games. When the game pauses to reload, they eat handfuls of trail mix. They go through a week's worth of snacks in mere hours. It really grates on my nerves.

Something had to be done. The specimens were self-destructing. It wouldn't be long before Specimen 2 would start smoking.

My anger swells as I slip on a lab coat and fill it with hypodermic needles. I descend the staircases towards the basement.

By the time I reach Specimen 2's suite, my knuckles are white with fury. I can't contain the resentment I feel towards these sloths or, rather, towards myself. They've lost their spark. The substance that made them so intriguing. Now they were ordinary men again. Nothing to write papers about.

Yet it was my fault. The electrodes, the serums, the programming. Something was slipping. Were batteries dying? Maybe some of the electrodes were growing faulty over all this time.

Preparations would have to be made to examine the electrodes thoroughly. They would have to be sleeping during the examination.

"What is going on here?" I asked as I barreled through the door.

"What do you mean?" they asked.

"Why aren't you working? Or training? Or doing something?"

"What's wrong, Doc? Something wrong?"

"Miriam, get a grip."

"Look at you two. What's going on?"

They looked at each other and laughed.

"What? We're not the hot, young studs you hoped we'd forever be?" Specimen 1 chided.

"Maybe we want to relax for once," Specimen 2 said, stretching his arms over his head.

"Not much point living anyway, at least in these conditions," Specimen 1 said.

"You have everything you ever needed. A home. Career. Food. Video games!" I yelled.

"We don't have freedom, Doc. Perhaps you've forgotten that, since you come and go as you please," Specimen 1 said.

"You have all that you need and I would appreciate some gratefulness," I said.

"Oh, is it time for another needle, Doc?" Specimen 1 taunted me as he reached for my jacket pocket. With barely any time to think, I squeezed the bracelet. Both men fell to the ground, screaming in agony, clutching their balls.

"Smarten up," I shouted as I left them writhing on the ground. I stomped out of the room and locked it for the night. I'm sure they have no idea why I was so furious. They have no idea how badly off the rails this train is going.

What in the formula is causing the weight gain? Which protocol is triggering their inability to care?

The drops? The vibrations? The currents? The pitch? The frequency?

Again I have to restructure.

*Specimen 3*

The time for integration was drawing near. Specimen 3 was pretty much dancing on my last nerve, so it was time to make the jump. The idea of moving my specimens to the next phase often disturbed me. It was the final line of morality crossed by me to benefit science with my discoveries.

Beauty, stamina, intelligence—all experienced in their purest forms, or at least the closest I could come in the environment in which I was working.

No one knew she was with me. She, too, was locked in the cell of Internet vacancy and none of her messages reached the outside world.

She was from another country, on the road more often than not. It would be weeks before anyone would even consider searching for her. And they'd never suspect she was anywhere but in California, as I let her more innocuous tweets originate from fake California IP addresses.

Even if she had told anyone about me when we were flirting, and even if she had told them she was coming to see me, that was so long ago. Her persona had been jet-setting and conducting interviews and posing for photo shoots all this time, even if half of them were just ideas that I made up on my own.

"My darling," I said loudly in an affected voice as I strutted into her bedroom. Specimen 3 had been examining her face in front of the vanity and turned to face me.

"What is it, Miriam?" she asked, brushing her long, currently orange, straight hair.

"I've been thinking how hard everything has been for all of us lately," I said as I walked behind her and hugged her. We both studied our faces in the mirror. I had short, blonde hair this day and it went well with her long, orange hair. We made a lovely couple.

"We need to get away together. Just you and me," I whispered.

"Just you and me?" She smiled. "I'd like that."

"I've booked us for four days at the Port Perry Spa Resort." I grinned.

"I love that place, and it's been so long since we've gone."

"I know. I'm sorry. I wanted the best for you and this is going to be our new beginning."

"I'm so happy." She spun around and stood up to hug me. We kissed and her excitement was infectious. We spent the rest of the afternoon enjoying each other in her satin sheets. For a few brief hours, my goddess pleased me on every level. When it was nighttime and I was making my notes, I almost didn't want to proceed with the plan.

But I did.

*Journal*

While I planned the weekend retreat to the last detail (which are outlined in the other journals), I readied the boys for several days in a coma.

I wasn't sure what else to do with them, for to leave them unguarded for that long would surely be a folly I couldn't risk.

With the boys slipped back into suspended animation, I packed for my trip.

*Specimen 3*

I'd taken her several times to the spa to prepare for when the end of the experiment would come. When I first had her, I truly thought I could never live without her.

But then, the glamour girl was gone. This was a pudgy, whiney, self-absorbed baby who had no sense of goddess about her at all anymore.

Once we arrived at the retreat, I led her to the bar and then to the mud baths. We changed into our robes, and I looked at her naked, gleaming body one last time, and I remember the girl with the butterfly painted across her chest. We were escorted to tubs of warm mud that were separated by a little bench where you could disrobe. We were helped into the warm, thick clay by the assistants and we sank into it with delight.

While in the baths, we sipped champagne. Hers was tainted with a specific formula. Mine was delicious.

"Are you enjoying yourself?" I asked her.

"Most definitely," she said. "I'm tipsy already."

I had secretly arranged for a telephone call to be made to the attendant during the time that we were bathing.

Specimen 3 lay back in her tub of muck, her words slurred as she tipped yet another glass of champagne down her throat.

"I'm glad I met you, Doctor," she said. "Even though you're weird."

"I'm glad we met too," I said, leaning back in the mud.

She was kind, and I almost felt sorry to say goodbye.

"You know, the best way to enjoy the bath is to hold your breath and sink down under. Keep your whole body down as long as you can. It'll clean out your pores better than any cleanser."

"Okay," she said as she sank down.

The drugs coursing through her system gave her no sense of time or instinct or common sense. She lay under the mud for a while and then her hands flung up out of the bath. She started to rise up out of the mud, hands reaching out and clawing at the sides of the tub. I watched from my own tub, sipping my champagne, wondering how much of this event was playing on the security cameras.

Mud was flung around as she tried to rise from her tub. She panicked, sucking in even more through her nose and mouth. She coughed on her mud, and I watched her. Mud bubbled from her mouth and nose. She wiped at her eyes only to smear more mud so that she couldn't see. She flailed one last time until she was still. Her body slid back into the mud.

I slowly stepped out of the tub; being covered in warm mud with a champagne head rush makes it a dangerous business, so I had to be very careful. I went over to Specimen 3 and hauled her limp, heavy, mud-clad body from the tub. I laid her down on the floor, and cleared her nose and mouth. Then I carefully stepped over to the desk, leaving clumps of mud in my wake, and rang for an attendant.

"Hello?" I called out, my voice frantic. "Can anyone help us? Help us!"

I waited for a while, pulled at Specimen 3 again, slapping at her face, turning her over to let the mud roll off of her.

"Anyone?" I screamed as I pressed the emergency bell again. The only sound was the miniwaterfall crashing beside me.

It was five minutes before anyone came and Specimen 3 was long dead.

The attendant was rightfully horrified and couldn't imagine what happened. It wasn't my fault no one heard the bell that I rang several times. I played the distraught partner very well, hysterical in my grief. But nothing would bring back my beauty.

It was a relief.


*Journal*

I asked the funeral home to ship the body to me at the university morgue until I was able to locate a relative to take her body.

At the university, I was able to take several molds of her body in several positions for various classroom studies. I was actually getting a reputation of casting better molds than some of the big companies who were rushed and careless. My molds were carefully crafted from the specimens. Over the years, I'd explored several techniques to replicate the living. Many of my attempts resulted in perfection as magnificent as any mortuary or Hollywood FX team.

Building up inventory, while slipping in two molds to take to my home laboratory for my own devices, was normal protocol. All the bases had been covered years ago. My portfolio. My creatures.

Once I had replicated the beautiful creature who lay in repose in the coffin, I was able to perform a sleight of hand for the security cameras. The illusion was that I had taken home two artificial bodies, not one fake and one real.

Specimen 3 floats in a pool of fluids, the components of which are detailed more thoroughly in my other journal. The implants still pulse, multiple tubes pierce her in various parts of her body, a labyrinth linking her life flow to a computer. Her beauty is all around me, filtered through the electrodes and pulsing into my own bloodstream. She is here, only her soul is gone. The heart has stopped for now.

Even now, as I write in this journal, I can feel her long, slender fingers tickling the back of my neck, sending shivers up and down my spine in that playful manner unique to her.

"I wish it hadn't come to this," I told her as I stared at her floating in her fluid. "It's my fault. I grew sloppy." So entranced with my own grandeur because of my success with the first two specimens that I had miscalculated with the third one, for the female hormones, for the hollow lack of empathy.

*Specimen 3*

She had been immersed in the fluids for long enough without proceeding with the experiment. I had needed time to think and catch my breath. As I get older, it seems to take longer and use up more energy to do the tasks that came so easily in my youth. However, after more pondering, I was up to the task to begin the next phase.

It was time to slowly reprogram her essence back into her physical body. I turned on the MP3 player, the surround sound in the room cranked at full blast. Multiple speakers were attached to the glass and sometimes the water would tremble slightly if a piece with heavy bass was routing through the system, both on the overhead system and through the water. She was being bathed in the new program.

Her flesh twitched and tremored where the multiple electrodes were affected, jerking like a frog-leg experiment. I hummed along as I made notes about the recordings and vital signs in the other journal. It would take an indeterminably long time for the switchover to happen. It might be days, weeks, perhaps even months. Patience is one skill that I need to continue to hone in order to persevere with these experiments.

The fluids were mostly a conducting gel that gently routed the electromagnetic currents to various parts of her body. Her brain was being rerouted, new paths for the synapses to fire on. Her heart began to vibrate once more. One tremor at a time. A false life. An illusion created by machinery and technology. The first trick would be capturing her essence. The second trick, if at all possible, if time and money and patience would allow, would be to see if she could be salvaged and reprogrammed with a new essence.

The second part I am completely skeptical about, never seeing reports or even hints of success in any papers, books, blogs or journals that I'd ever read. Sure, there was the reattaching of limbs, growing a few new body parts, cloning and the like. But if I removed her essence, could she be reanimated, and if so, what would she be like? I am completely skeptical that anyone has attempted the exact experiment that I am contemplating, once this first experiment is complete.

After fourteen hours there were small changes. Limbs moved slowly in the fluids like an embryo in the uterus. She was breathtaking and I photographed her many times.

I framed one of the pictures and hung it in my bedroom. The photograph shows her face in sweet repose, lips demure, high, sharp cheekbones and, somehow, an air of innocence. Sleeping Beauty in her crypt. The photograph is blurry because of the fluids which give the observer a sense of being underwater. There were two tiny cables entwining, floating by the side of her face, woven from the bottom of the picture towards the top. It was as if she was being born all over again, the fluids both giving and removing her life force.

Captured in that one photographic moment was all that I loved and despised in my beauty.

*Journal*

Specimens 1 and 2 are bored and boring. No matter what combinations I try, the initial *joie de vivre* isn't there. Sure, they still fuck like rock stars and that's why it's always so difficult to make logical decisions.

I grow weary of their day-to-day routines. Specimen 1 does his weird hours of writing, Specimen 2 is off at the crack of dawn to jog or bike or swim. Around nine o'clock at night, we fuck for a couple of hours or go clubbing. I go back to research. Specimen 1 goes back to writing. Specimen 2 goes to bed.

Wash. Rinse. Repeat

The point isn't settling.

The point is perfection.

And one person's perfection isn't another's.

How do you activate the part of the brain that makes a person perceive perfection?

And what do you do when your idea of perfection mutates?


To them, the boys, they have perfection. They watch TV and play video games to their hearts' content, eating and drinking at will, indulging in their muses for a time and getting fucked on a regular basis in various ways.

But this is my world and my perfection. These are not the men that stirred lust in me. These men have become complacent, and in turn, so have I.

And I must not settle.

I don't want to send them into the next phase of the experiment just yet. I can't let either one of them go until I'm certain it will be a success.


*Journal*

My specimens utterly exhaust me. For two days and two nights, I had nothing to do with any of them. I drugged and shackled them, and there they will stay until I'm ready to soldier on.

I need the break. Tending to them is exhausting and thankless. My mind needs to focus on other stimuli to refresh. Even someone as focused as me can suffer burnout.

For nearly forty-eight hours, I left my bedroom suite only to rummage for food in the kitchen to put into my room fridge. A few bottles of red wine were also brought in. The bed was the perfect sanctuary and so were the specialty stations that my big-screen TV was showing. I lost myself in old movies—*King Kong*, several versions of *Frankenstein*, a few *Dracula*s and *Creature Features*. I moved on to Marilyn Monroe's *Seven Year Itch* and then a Shirley Temple movie. I ate poorly, drank too much booze, smoked too much pot and thought of nothing but what was on the screen before me.

Once I had my brain-cleansing decompression session, I was ready to move forward.

My biggest issue is that I'm falling prey to my lust again.

I want something exciting to happen, and everything is routine and boredom now. This is how it always turns out.

Since I'm in charge and what I say goes, there's no sense of surprise or playfulness.

Is the answer truly to start the search again? Does this mean that the experiment is a failure?

Though I've not completed the next phase yet, it's still too early to know if the experiment could be a success. However, do I have the passion to carry on with my current specimens?

*Journal*

I made the decision as I stood in the shower, the pelting of hot water on my skull pounded in another component to my experiment. I needed to find a new specimen. It was time to stir the pot. So the combination of beauty, brains and brawn didn't work out this time. Perhaps I'm very close to another combination. Or maybe I'm missing an element I'd not considered before. There is always so much more to learn the very minute that we believe that we've unlocked the puzzle.

Instead of presenting to myself a detailed schemata of who the next specimen would be, I'd let fate decide. Perhaps I'd choose the first one I meet. Perhaps I'd need to examine several possibilities until I decided on the next honored guest in my sacred family.

Once I pampered myself with a day of self-mani-pedis, lounged around in a terry-cloth robe dying my hair a one-off magenta, the plan began to formulate in my mind.

I returned to the sex club. This time, I was solo.

From the moment I showed up at the door, I was greeted warmly, as if I were the most important person in town. The doorman knew me by name, the desk clerk gave me my single-lady bracelet and I didn't even have to pay. Ladies night. Fate was on my side.

I stood staring around the club, happy to see many single guys walking around. There appeared to be a few options.

The idea was to add a component into the family that had been missing. I had three but in my haste to begin my research, I didn't consider in any real detail that there are always more and how our yearning for components mutates. Should there be more finance? How about an artist? Perhaps a computer programmer would be most handy with all of my equipment.

The cosmopolitans went down easy and soon the dance floor was flush with pickings. Sure, everyone was milling around this early in the night, but soon there would be dancing.

Standing at the bar, waiting for another cosmo to be made, a tall, buff, scruffy, blond guy with multiple earrings and tattoos stood very close to me. He had a very young face.

"You're new," he said, with a not-quite-convincing façade.

"I beg to differ," I said. "You're the one who's new."

He took a sip of his drink.

"Are you even old enough to drink, young man?" I whispered to him playfully.

"I love to play with cougars," he said with a smile.

He bought me a drink, which actually surprised me, but I gave him points for having manners.

"What's your name?" I asked him.

"Brad," he said. "What's yours?"

"Miriam." We shook hands and laughed. We stepped away from the bar, towards the dance floor which was beginning to fill with couples gyrating lasciviously. I watched a couple, regulars I'd played with many times, in front of us dirty dancing. The man was snaking his hand right up his wife's legs, under her miniskirt and into her G-string. The boy stared at the couple as if watching his first porn movie.

"What do you do? Are you still in high school?" I teased, running my fingers along his firm bicep. His hair smelled fresh and fruity, with a dash of musk and a bit of nervous sweat. The smell of prey, ripe for the picking. Is this the type of specimen I need or will he just be a toy for the night?

"I'm done with high school. In fact, did a year of college, but now I'm freelancing."

"Oh really? Doing what?" The couple in front of us was now necking, the man's hands massaging her ass while they rocked into each other to the chants of Lady Gaga. They looked at me. I smiled. I remembered them, Cassandra and Felix, and raised my glass in a toast. I turned my focus back to Specimen 4.

"I'm a musician," he said rather sheepishly.

"Oh… So how can you afford to pay one hundred twenty dollars to come in here on ladies' night, not to mention the ten-bucks-a-pop drinks?"

"I'm a session musician. When big groups come to town, they hire locals and I get steady work. Bands and movies are my gigs. Sometimes a commercial. Of course, I also play my guitar in a nightclub. But it's not my only trick. I play a lot of instruments."

His face had become so animated, his enthusiasm as he spoke of his passion hoisted his energy, and his charisma overwhelmed me. The scent of his passion enthralled me as Madonna moaned her way through "Justify My Love" and I leaned over as if to kiss him. Instead, I turned my head and looked back at the dance floor.

"Let's dance," I said, pulling him toward it.

"Oh no, I'm no good at that stuff," he protested.

"A musician? Who can't dance?"

"I play it, I don't do it," he whined as I pulled him towards the dance floor.

He danced very well, gyrating his sexy pelvis. We danced closer to the couple we'd been watching. Before long, the four of us were writhing together to the beat. I kissed Cassandra and the men danced around us. Cassandra and I ran our hands along each other's bodies, our fingers coyly lifting each other's skirts so that the onlookers could see our lingerie. Before long, the four of us retreated to the back rooms.

Specimen 4 was very shy in the locker room. It was rather adorable, because of how young he was. Everyone has a first time and tonight was his, although he didn't admit it. He tried not to stare around him at the dozen or so people stripping naked. I peeled off my outfit and neatly folded my clothes, putting them in a locker. Once the four of us were naked, with our towels wrapped around us, we walked into the upstairs bar area.

We bought a round of drinks, using our reputations as collateral on a tab, and wandered through the open-area orgy room. Several mattresses were on the floor and a Jacuzzi was nearby where many naked people lounged with martinis. Beyond the Jacuzzi were washrooms with hangers, more lockers, mirrors and shelves with all kinds of toiletries, including wet wipes, condoms, lube, mouthwash, mints, latex gloves and more. Since we had no purses, it was nice to be able to have access to such products.

When the four of us had finished our drinks, we went to another level of the club where drinks weren't allowed for safety reasons. There were many rooms with beds, one had a spanking bench, another had a doctor's table, still another had a sex swing.

Specimen 4 stared at the swing.

"Have you ever used one?" I asked him, enjoying the look of anticipation and excitement as he puzzled over the logistics of it.

"No," he said. He was adorable as he stared at the swing, his hand holding his towel primly over his growing erection.

"Do you want to see?" I asked him. I didn't wait for a reply as I slid myself into the swing with the help of Cassandra and Felix. It took a few minutes for me to get my balance and then I was ready for my close-up.

"Now, you come to me and fuck me," I said. He stared at me.

"Right now?" he asked.

"Sure, right now. First get one of those condoms from that urn, and then come and swing me."

He didn't say a word as he looked around. We saw an orgy undulating on the bed near us, and the cries and thumps of good, hard fucking filled the air. There was jazzy music playing, but it was very low and nonintrusive on this level. As he fumbled with the condom, I smiled.

"Come here," I said. He didn't need much coaxing for me to help him get hard with my mouth. I rocked the swing gently and soon he got the hang of getting a blow job from someone in a swing. He even relaxed enough to use my breasts as leverage for controlling the swing.

I turned my head from him so that I could speak.

"Now, fuck me," I commanded.

He began to fuck me. Cassandra was on her knees, giving Felix head while they watched us on the swing.

I watched Specimen 4's face as he fucked me. His youthful vitality flowed with every rhythmic thrust of his hips. His body locked with mine in a magnificent way, filling me and giving me shudders of pleasure that I had long missed. A crowd was forming, watching this magnificent musician copulating with the cougar on the swing. Even though it was business as usual at the sex club, for newcomers it was quite a party trick.

"We'd better let someone else have a turn," I told him as I noticed a couple of ladies giving me the eye that my time had expired. He helped me from the swing and I showed him where to put his used condom and pointed out some wet wipes.

The four of us ventured on through the club maze, stopping to watch an orgy or a threesome, and then moving on. There was another Jacuzzi on this level and there were four people lounging in it. You weren't allowed to actually have sex in it for health-code reasons although, considering what was going on all around, it didn't really seem like it should matter. But it did, so people respected the code.

There was a room that was all bed and mirrors. The light was so dim you could hardly see the mirrors, so it seemed kind of pointless. We made sure there were condoms and wet wipes in the room and then set to work making out with each other. This time, I kissed Felix, and Cassandra kissed Specimen 4. Then we swapped.

Cassandra went down on me, her skilled little tongue taking me places where there were no experiments or agendas. For the first time in months, I didn't have to worry about the bracelet or someone disappearing on me. I only had to worry about myself.

I sucked Specimen 4's cock and Felix played with my breasts, and more couples filled the bed with us. Groping hands and probing cocks thrilled me in the darkness. Lips kissed me everywhere—men, women—it was a blur. The music was faint, an old big-band, saucy piece, and my mind released into the experience of full-body sensation.

My animal side emerged—my senses sharp, my nails long, my teeth itching to taste salty flesh, to lick and suck a creature until it quivers with delight under my mercy. Then it was my turn to take what is mine—all flesh, all blood, all taste, all mind...

The night was a blur of constant sex. Sweaty, passionate, needy sex. There was something in the air that night; the entire club possessed an urgent air about it. As if something was going to happen, a buzz of erotic anticipation, perhaps a full moon or other planetary alignment. More than usual, people were reaching out to each other, exploring beyond their boundaries as men touched men and women were sandwiched in between. I don't know how many partners I had or how many rooms I dragged Specimen 4 through. He had a big grin on his face all night as he banged lady after lady on our mission of lust.

One time, as I went into the bathroom, Cassandra greeted me on the way out. "Stall three," she whispered, "behind the toilet tank. Try it."

I peeked behind the tank and there was a little cloth satchel looking like a piece of trash wedged in the back. I pulled it out and there was a vial of coke, a small spoon, a razor blade and a little mirror. Still a half vial left.

I helped myself to a couple of lines and the night continued on in lusty frenzy.

As I went home in the taxi by myself, the orange rays of dawn stretching across the fading night sky, I dreamed of a life where I didn't have to worry about micromanaging specimens, one in which I'd at last hit upon the proper combination so that everything works as it should. The evening had been one of those magical nights.

It was rare for the club to be that vibrant in such a specific way. Certainly it was always a steamy, seductive atmosphere, but the ambiance of tonight had been slightly different. The combinations of lust and personalities had worked so well. I saw no tears, no jealousy, no drama. A welcome relief on all levels, I'm sure, for the bouncers too. People had slipped from partner to partner in an unseen dance of unspoken consent. Condoms were used, of course, and always a fresh one for each partner. It was different to dance with strangers such as this, in the dark, with no worry but getting to the next orgasm.

Specimen 4 had fit right in, dancing right along with me, learning the steps and small courtesies quickly and efficiently. He brought me water and towels. He was polite to the partners. He didn't overwhelm anyone, but just let the night unfold.

It was a bit depressing to put him in a cab and send him home. But I knew it wouldn't be long before our paths crossed again.

The rising sun was a spotlight on me as I fumbled with the front door, illuminating the doctor stumbling in after dawn once more.

I was revitalized and ready to proceed.

*Specimen 1*

Once again, Specimen 1 has fallen asleep in front of the TV with a drink in his hand. I write this staring at him with contempt. I'm trying to remember that first lusty time in the staff bathroom at faculty. How he had thrilled me to no end with his touch and looks and smell. His newness. His accent.

He is so familiar now. Sometimes I despise him.

*Journal*

The latest preparations have been completed.

## Specimen 1

I stood in the doorway of Specimen 1's office, wearing a new red leather corset with black piping, accented with brass buckles and giving me impressive cleavage. I wore thigh-high red leather boots that had six-inch spikes. Long red fingerless gloves showed off my new red claws. For a change of pace, a long curly blonde wig and a red riding crop crowned my look.

Specimen 1 stopped typing to give me the once-over. He grinned. Like clockwork, he stopped what he was doing and came over to me, hugging and kissing me, nuzzling the new leather all over. I pushed him back haughtily then took his hand. I led him to a mock bathroom I had pulled together on the main floor, a flat-board stage replica of the bathroom we had shared that first lusty night.

"What is this?" he asked me.

"Do you recognize it?" I asked him, unbuttoning his shirt.

"I do, but why?" he asked as he helped me get his shirt and pants off.

"I thought maybe it would be fun to relive that first night…"

"Anything you desire, Doctor," he said as he kissed me.

Oh, we relived those glorious moments and it was nearly as thrilling as it had been back then. We used the chair, the couch, the floor, just as we had that first night. His face was happy as we spoke the words we had spoken that night. Excitement grew for both of us as the distant memories of our first night reemerged into our present.

His hands caressed me with a passion I hadn't felt in a long time. A passion that felt like it was from his heart, not from my demands. His passion created new swells of longing and desire in me and I kissed him.

"Miriam, what is wrong with you?" he asked me as he pulled back gently after a few moments.

"Nothing, why?" I asked, kissing his shoulders playfully.

"You're so passionate, you almost seem like you like me," he teased as he pushed his cock into me.

I groaned with pleasure. "Of course I like you, why do you think you're here…" I kissed him before he could answer and he rocked into me with fresh abandon. We both cried and moaned as we rode our waves of pleasure that never seemed to end. We stopped and started so many times that it was morning by the time we were finished. The sun shone through the top slats of the living room's drapes and I realized I'd lost yet another night to sex. How will my work ever be done?

We both finally stood up from where we snuggled on the floor, helping each other and then hugging.

My heart beat against his as we stood there. In the reflection of one of the many mirrors, I caught the gaze of his tortured blue eyes. I still want to crawl into his eyes and see what is really in his soul. I held him close and relished his lean warmth of bone and flesh.

I wondered if he ever thought about what his life had been before he met me.

*Journal*

The glow of my re-creation with Specimen 1 was short-lived. Again, the dull rhythm of complacency was the backbeat to our three lives. I had my own career and then I also had to keep up the public façade of theirs. It was exhausting and getting boring. I satisfied myself with the fact that things always change. And I was just waiting.

Our routines had become predictable, even when we tried different sex clubs, our routines were the same. It was partly because I had to have so much control over them. I longed for the freedom of not worrying about them escaping or telling. One wrong word in the bathroom and I would be done for.

I look at both of them, and though they do nothing wrong and they obey the rules, now that the goddess is gone, I can't get past the sense of "is this all there is?".

The perfection I strive for did exist for a short time, but I hadn't factored in the emotional elements.

How boring perfection can be.

Change is necessary.

The experiment has been not quite a failure, but not quite a success either. It has certainly given me some observations and benchmarks that I hadn't quite considered before.

The human element. The brainwashed don't get bored, but the one doing the brainwashing does.

*Specimen 2*

He fills me with ennui. No matter what I do, his focus is on his races and his lady fans. Adjusting the formulas has made him more driven to win than ever before, his idea of perfection. He wants to conquer the world, win every triathlon that he can enter, bang every pretty young triathlete that catches his eye. His interest in me feels the most false, the most manufactured. My interest in his usefulness for this phase of my experiments has pretty much expired.

"I have a surprise for you," I told Specimen 2 as I entered his home gym. He was lifting weights, his tight-muscled ass jutting out as he slowly stood under the pressure.

"What is it?" he huffed as he reached full height. He slowly lowered the weights again and then raised the bar above his head before putting it down heavily. It was the best decision to keep his gym equipment in his massive bedroom. He didn't have a several-room suite as Specimen 1 does, but slamming that kind of weight down in an old house like this would likely result in the barbells going right through the floor. At least down here we were on solid concrete that went down four feet. I know because I have several spots where I've put squirrel nests with important documents, spare keys, data, and other valuable information and goods. I had this floor specially poured a few years ago after my experiments became more secretive and more high stakes.

"I'm sending you to San Francisco," I said. "I can't go because I have to give two lectures next week."

"Why am I going to San Francisco?"

"So you can participate in the Escape from Alcatraz triathlon."

His eyes widened in delight.

"You're letting me enter?"

"Letting you? You're already signed up, come and see."

I went over to his desk and sat down in his chair. Since his computer was already on, it only took a second to load the Escape from Alcatraz triathlon dummy page that I had replicated from the original. Oh yes, he was going, his name was the same in real life as in the shell. He was definitely participating in Alcatraz.

Part of me wanted to go there with him. To stand on the pier staring out at Alcatraz Island, watching thousands of eager triathletes swimming towards San Francisco. I'd been to San Francisco several times and knew how mysterious that fog was and the secrets it could hide. How steep those roads were, and all those triathletes had to bike their way up and down those windy roller coasters. It would be a good race.

I needed to stay in Toronto. I couldn't be flying to San Francisco with Specimen 2. It was much too risky.

Everything I prepared was with the utmost delicate care. There could be zero room for forensic signs of sabotage. There could be no room for detection or error.

The implants needed to be programmed to pass the Customs detection machines and any other searches that might occur at the border and the marathon.

He needed to be programmed to not talk about us, the tongue implant burning him if he says anything at all out of line. I would be monitoring through my phone and computers and other surveillance equipment.

I need to ramp the stamina strain to the upmost frequency so that it can be captured. If it's possible to capture and save.


The triathlon was to be televised on a specialty pay station that I could get through a US cable system. Specimen 1 and I sat down to watch how he'd fare. Specimen 1 didn't know I could hear everything that Specimen 2 said through my earpiece and I could watch whom he was speaking with through a tiny camera in his swimming attire.

The triathletes were all on the ferry, eagerly waiting for it to chug out to the designated spot, already shivering from the cold ocean breeze through their bathrobes. Birds called, piercing through my headpiece. I hoped Specimen 1 couldn't hear but he was engrossed in the big-screen TV, trying to spot Specimen 2 in the throngs.

The camera panned across the athletes and we caught a quick glimpse of Specimen 2 staring out at the water with firm concentration.

I fiddled with some buttons on my cell phone. Specimen 1 looked over at me.

"I can't believe you're texting when the race is about to begin."

"It hasn't begun yet." I smiled.

The boat reached its destination and soon the diving began. The water was filled with triathletes swimming towards the San Francisco Harbor. I clicked my cell phone buttons again. The camera panned across the water. The announcer suddenly had panic in his voice.

"Oh my God, off to the left, there is a dorsal fin. A large dorsal fin. And it's headed right for the swimmers."

Whistles were blown in panic and some of the swimmers turned to look. A great white shark breached the water with an athlete in its mouth. There were screams as blood filled the water. Swimmers raced toward the boat, clawing over each other as they blindly flailed. Two more dorsal fins appeared and more great whites breached the water with hapless swimmers in their mouths.

The sharks feasted on the athletes like popcorn, the water a slick red, athletes, dripping blood, pulled onto the boat by panicked volunteers.

In my ear, there had been shrieking and crying and then the feed stopped. For a second after the TV coverage stopped, Specimen 2 screamed in my ear, water crashing against the mic. And then there was nothing.

Specimen 1 was frantically trying to find CNN to see what Anderson Cooper would have to say about the attacks. At last, he found it in time to see a breaching shark being replayed.

"That's insane," Specimen 1 said. "Oh my God. Do you think he's okay?"

"I guess we'll find out, if he can get to a phone. It looks like they're trying to organize them to check in."

A URL was flashed along the bottom of the screen, a site where triathletes who had checked in after the accident could be identified.

I clicked to the URL on my phone and as CNN babbled on in the background, I repeatedly refreshed the screen. Specimen 2's name never appeared.

"You're so cold," Specimen 1 said suddenly. "He was our friend. I know you didn't like him much near the end, but you're the one that brought him here."

"Yes, I brought him here. Don't you think I'm in shock? I just might have possibly seen my lover, a man I did truly love, just get eaten by a shark. Pretty random for city folk, don't you think?"

"I bet you had something to do with this. How many times does this happen? Probably never, or they wouldn't keep having this race, would they? I bet you put those sharks there."

Specimen 1 went and retrieved another beer from the fridge and sat back down.

"How on earth would I put sharks in San Francisco Harbor from Toronto?"

"Oh, I don't know. Maybe you just picked up a phone and had the Mafia dump some sharks there."

"No wonder you're a writer, you have a pretty vivid imagination. It was a horrible accident, that's all."

"Yes, a horrible accident," he muttered.

We watched CNN a bit longer and we didn't speak of it again.


*Specimen 4*

It took me a few days between my professional obligations to soundproof one of the larger attic rooms and install some wiring. The ceiling had been bare so it wasn't too hard to hammer the boards onto the beams. Most of the room was of a sufficient height that he could play the guitar as long as he didn't go all Pete Townshend with a jumping windmill. I hauled speaker systems up. Luckily, modern technology weighed a couple of thousand pounds less than speakers, amps and other gear of ancient times. It truly was a marvel how quickly music technology had shifted even within my own lifetime. I had to install many hidden cameras and microphones, of course.

By the time I was finished, the attic was furnished in such a way that it looked like it'd been a studio for at least a decade. Worn couches, guitars on the walls, mic stands, mic, glass case, a violin, several percussion instruments, not to mention a drum kit.

The room was set up so that one end was a small area to resemble a coffee-house stage. The flooring was different, a special black stage flooring. The drum kit was set back, and there was a small lighting grid with little colored lights that you could change with a foot pedal on the drum kit or by switches on a wall panel.

When Specimen 4 entered my attic room his mouth hung open. He walked around, staring into the glass cases at various precious instruments, framed autographs and programs of rock stars, and didn't notice how I double-locked the door behind him.

I clicked a switch on a wall panel beside the door. Music filled the room, a steady beat of primal drumming, the echoing twang of electric guitars. Of course it was specially programmed music created for Specimen 4. I turned it down so that it was merely background ambiance. I indicated a wooden table where he could lay his guitar case. When he set down the case, he looked around some more.

"What's a scientist doing with such a rocking place?" he finally stammered. "Aren't you guys all nerdy and stuff?"

"I like to rock out now and again, as do my friends. It's how we grew up." I laughed at him and touched his arm.

"Let me watch you play guitar," I said.

He trembled as he unlatched the case and brought out the guitar. It didn't strike me that he was nervous about playing for me. No, he was a sensitive musician type and his spidey senses were tingling. His nervousness had nothing to do with his guitar.

"Are you nervous, darling?" I asked him. "How about a beer to calm your nerves?"

His face brightened. "Yes, ma'am." He nodded.

"Ma'am?" I raised an eyebrow and gave him a doubtful look.

"I mean, thanks, Miriam."

I went over to the small bar fridge that I'd managed to haul up the stairs with a pulley-lever contraption. My strength gave me more freedom than most. While Specimen 4 tuned his guitar and paced around the small stage area, I opened two beers and watched him. His long, curly hair was a refreshing change and the strumming of his guitar sent chills down my back, and he wasn't even plugged in yet. I brought him the beer and we set up the frequencies for his guitar to go through my system.

I turned off the background music and then sat behind the drum kit.

"So what do you want to play?" I asked.

"How about 'Highway to Hell'?" he said.

I laughed. "Let's do it," I clicked my sticks together and we managed to perform a not-too-crappy version of the old AC/DC anthem. We played a few more songs, drinking several beers in between. I also added other instruments through the various systems. At one point, we sounded like ELO. It was a great amusement and diversion.

Music does create a vibration through the bones that nothing else in life does. Perhaps music was one of the keys that were missing. Yes, I used the music to hypnotize all of them, but perhaps an elixir of genetic musicality was what was required for the cocktail.

We sat on the couch, taking a break from our jam, and stared at the drum kit.

"What do you see happening next for you?" I asked him, running my hand up his thigh towards his crotch.

"You mean, like, in my life?"

"Of course, darling…" My hand cupped his crotch. He smiled and blushed.

"Well, of course it would be great to be a rock star but I see what's involved. There's a chance I may get a kick at the can, being in the right place at the right time, but of course, there's always the whole specter of failure and nothingness mocking me too."

"Whenever I have moments of self-doubt, I remind myself, if I don't believe in me, who else is going to believe in me?" I shared with him.

"That's a good one."

"That's how I get through life and that's why I have dozens of awards for ground-breaking experimentation."

My hand snaked up his chest, my fingers unbuttoning his shirt. He shifted on the couch, leaning his head back, staring up at the ceiling.

"I need more…" His words slurred and stopped. I looked at his eyes; they were closed. I took the bottle of beer from his hand before he could spill it. He was beginning to snore.

The drug in his beer was producing the required effect and it was going to be all too easy.

I lay him out on the couch. It didn't take long to remove his clothes. It wasn't time to implant yet. He had to be programmed with the headset first.

Once his brain waves reach a specific frequency, I can add the implants.

The couch back clicked down so that he was on a bed and the couch arms were head- and footboards. Embedded in both sides of the inside paneling of the couch were shackles for his hands and feet.

I cleaned up our mess, put his guitar away and so on, keeping an eye on his vital signs as the headphones piped in the instructions to his cellular structure.

He was so sweet, lying on the couch. Before I shackled him, I crawled on top of him and kissed him. His soft, sweet lips kissed back—he was half-asleep, but not. His hands roamed down my back, feeling my curves beneath my clothes. Even though his eyes remained closed, his body was craving my touch.

I removed my clothes and removed his, careful not to knock the headphones from his ears. It was easy to slide onto his erection. I moved against him, slowly at first, afraid to wake him, but he was in a state of arousal in his sleep. The music was working as he thrust into me.

I sat up more and rode him until I was satisfied. He continued to thrust and we continued to copulate for quite some time. At last, I was exhausted and pulled myself away. Even as I dressed to leave him, he was still thrusting. I decided to turn down the coded music. Perhaps musicians don't need as strong a pulse there, as they are already so rhythmic. I made notes of the coordinates. He finally settled down and I left him.

I checked the cameras before I went to bed and he was asleep, his erection had spent at last during my journey towards bed.


Musicians have sexual stamina equivalent to athletes.


*Journal*

Once again, my dreams were laced with ferocious images. Specimen 3 creeps to my bedside, her flesh peeling, her eyes burning with both lust and hate. She'll stand there by my bed, her outline glowing eerily in the dim moonlight. Is she a dream? An energy surge? My guilty conscience?

She reaches for me, her hands rotting. I can smell the stench of death on her, can hear the clattering of her bones as she stretches her arm, then she sputters and sparks, as if she's an old-fashioned TV tube. The muddy smell of musk and seaweed creates a nausea so vile that I need my bathroom quickly. But the creature is there, standing there. Staring at me with accusing eyes.

"What do you want?" I asked her.

She stared at me, eyes milky white, her skin molting as more bones were revealed. She opened her mouth as a high-pitched screeching noise flew out of her throat or stomach or somewhere else. The sound was so loud and high that I feared my eardrums would explode like crystal. I put my hands over my ears.

"Get out," I yelled, shutting my eyes, wishing her away like a child in a fairy tale.


Then came the dreams about Specimen 2.

They were always the same.

It was as if I was seeing through his eyes as events unfolded and, I guess, in a way I was, with all the equipment and recordings I had of his last moments.

First, he was sweating to death in his wet suit, surrounded by hundreds of other triathletes standing on the boat, chilly from the air, but slippery with sweat beneath their suits. Then they all jumped into the cold San Francisco water, starting their journey towards Alcatraz. He swam with the rest, but his body buzzed as bits of water seeped through the hundreds of pinpricks I had pierced into his wet suit. The salt water wormed its way into his implants with every stroke. He was way ahead of most of the others as his strong arms pulled him through the waves.

A darkness lurked below him, he could sense it before he really felt it. His dream arms grew paralyzed with fear as he noticed no other swimmers around him for miles. They were all scrambling back towards the boat as he flew into the air, hugged in the jaws of a great white like a little rag doll.

The shark toyed with him, tossing him out to sea and then snatching him up as it exploded from below him again. At last the shark was ready to eat for real and the sheer terror of staring at its gaping mouth coming towards him in the water like a torpedo always jerked me awake.

Upon my awakening, maybe after the fourth or fifth time, I was aware that he was there with me too.

Not really as a ghost. Just as sharp flashes of images and impulses. He was drawn to my own implants, even after death, as was the beauty.

*Specimen 1*

He seems to be content writing and drinking. He's lonely with Specimen 2 gone.

I thought about Specimen 2 trying to claw his way out of some shark's belly. I can't help but feel a little bit of glee when I think about how Specimen 2 snuck around with the goddess behind my back.

Specimen 1 hasn't said anything about how we're suddenly not fucking nightly and if he knows about Specimen 4 in the attic, he hasn't tipped his hand.


*Specimen 4*

There was a reason why I had settled on the thesis that a beauty, a brainiac and an athlete would be the best combination for the perfect lover. Since no *one* human is capable of perfection, combining the augmented quality of each with that of the others could possibly create perfection. Capturing all of their essence into a triad was possible with three bodies, but how would just the electrodes work together?

Adding a fourth to the chord had been a misguided experiment. The balance had been tedious enough to tend to, without the addition of a musician.

As it always happens to us mortals, the lure of the musician is a siren song difficult to elude. Curiosity always overrides common sense, there's something about their charisma, no matter who they are, that is alluring when their focus falls on you. Even I was charmed by the musician—the beauty of creating notes from strings and wood, and coaxing amazing sounds from throats and bows. Musicians were almost always the best lovers, likely because they were constantly moving anyways.

When musicians aren't making music or making love, they are worse than teenage girls. Mood swings, emotional outbursts, pouting withdrawals—it was exhausting. Even the athlete didn't pull the emotional blackmail that the musician did.

I was in a difficult spot. The musician was not going be a viable part of the experiment. However, I couldn't release him back into his former life. My brainwashing and programming talents weren't that skilled. He would tell people about me, no matter how much he might promise not to or fear repercussions should I discover it. He would never know how much power I could theoretically have over him for the rest of his life. I couldn't take any chances. I had to make certain that no one ever discovered anything at all that was happening in my home.

"Miriam…I think the neck of my guitar is warped, come look at it, please…" Specimen 4 whined from the bedroom. The tone of his voice made my skin crawl.

The spell was broken. The song is over for Specimen 4.


*Journal*

The house is old. That's the problem with these old gothic houses. Things can blow at any time, no matter how many renovations there are and how much new wiring rerouted—there will always be something missed. Old walls. Old wallpaper. Old curtains. You never know what is going to be a problem when it comes to an accident.

I lay sprawled naked across the couch while Specimen 4 played his guitar for me. It had been a good night—some wine, some sex, and now he serenaded me with a damn-fine rendition of "Hotel California". Just as he was hitting the chorus for the final refrain, there was a power surge. The lights flickered, the instruments glowed and made loud humming sounds while smoke and sparks flew everywhere. I stayed on my couch island as for several seconds the only sound was static electricity and Specimen 4 still holding his last note as his body shuddered and jolted along the floor like a puppet being dragged, his guitar still clutched in his frozen hands. Puffs of smoked wafted up from him, his guitar, the speakers...

Soon the noises all stopped. The smell of burned flesh filled the room so much that I thought the fire alarm would begin to bleat. The generator must have kicked in because some of the lights clicked and hummed back on as if nothing had happened, while all the instruments and lighting that had been on the same circuit didn't do anything at all. They were done.

In the end, the wiring couldn't withstand the electrical draw of all the equipment in the attic. The music room short-circuited, pretty straightforward. Once I was satisfied that the floor wasn't rife with electrical currents, I walked across the room to slip on a pair of his sneakers that were by the door.

I came back and stood over his body. It didn't twitch. It just lay there like a melted doll. He didn't even look real with his hair burned off in most places and half his face melted. His fingers had merged with the strings of his guitar. I wondered if his cock was seared to the melted guitar through his pants.

It was too bad it had to end like this. And I was glad I had thought ahead with the wiring, or so I thought, so that it would only affect this room.

It would be a while before he would be discovered missing.

So far, just in the time he'd been staying here, his disappearance hadn't been noted. I'd kept his online presence alive and well through a shell account that was untraceable, so there was no reason to believe anyone would discover him missing for a long time. Photoshop and text messaging were the best inventions to keep a person alive long after he wasn't. He could disappear anytime I willed him to disappear. That day would come, but not just yet.

First, there is the matter of disposing of his body. There's nothing to salvage from the melted mass of blood and guts that lay on my floor. It was like he had been cooked into a stew and then began to expand when the melting took over the inner pressure. It was going to be one hell of a mess to clean up. Not to mention equipment and wiring. If anyone came to check the house they would notice such things. I had a lot of work cut out for me.

*Specimen 1*

The mess in the attic would have to wait. I must be certain that the power surge only affected the attic and not the security systems or cameras. I hurried down the stairs to the basement, carrying hypodermic needles in my freshly donned lab coat, just in case there had been an escape.

All systems appeared to be secure. I entered the door to Specimen 1's office. His back was to me. As I walked closer, he appeared to be slumped over the computer.

"Oh no... Scott!" I cried out running towards him. The idea of him being gone was beyond belief. Yes, he was going to have to go too, they all did, but I hadn't been mentally prepared to let him slip from me in his current form just yet.

The choice had been made for me.

I looked at his body, determining the cause of death. Electrocution. When the power surge happened he was typing and for some reason there had been a jolt or short powerful enough to kill him. Likely a heart attack, since he wasn't burned or melted as Specimen 4 had been. Tears ran down my face as I pulled him from the keyboard. Whatever electrical currents had killed him were long gone from his system. Only his fingertips were singed.

"Oh, Scott," I cried as I dragged him from his chair and onto the floor. I lay him out and stared at him, his face clenched, his eye shut tight, as if he were on a scary ride.

Although his time was coming soon, this was too soon. I wasn't sure how I could adapt quickly.

"Enough," I scolded myself. I took several deep breaths and went over to Specimen 1's bar. I poured myself a large scotch. I went into my office and prepared the calculations.

Specimen 1 was easily wheeled from his room to the laboratory. First, I placed him on a slab to record all the necessary data and make the necessary speculative notes in the other journal. I stared at him. Forever still at last. Specimen 1 was gone. I hugged him and kissed his forehead.

"I'll see you on the other side," I whispered to him.

I began the process of running a myriad of tubes to and from various parts of him. Once everything was wired up, I wheeled him over to one of the tanks.


First, we stopped by Specimen 3. She floated on her back so beautifully, serene in the water, tubes rising from her like a myriad of seaweed strands. The perfect mermaid without a tail.

She must have felt us staring or maybe her electrodes were throbbing. She opened her eyes and turned her head to glare at us. The action caught me by surprise and I had to swallow before I stared back at her. She turned away from me, staring instead up at the ceiling.

I reminded myself she wasn't real, she hadn't even really looked. It was the electrical impulses making her body a puppet. She didn't breathe. She didn't see. She was dead.

"This will be you too, Scott," I said. I wheeled the bed to his tank. Carefully I moved him from the side bed to the stretched-out plastic over the tank. Once he was firmly in the middle, I cranked the wheel of the contraption that controlled the tension of the plastic tarp. Slowly he was lowered into the tank. I unhooked the plastic tarp from the one side of the tank and rolled it up on the other side with the crank.

Specimen 1 floated in the fluid while I affixed the wires that led from him into the machines.

Once I was satisfied that everything was functioning properly, I left him there.

*Specimen 1*

I slept in Specimen 1's room that night. My dreams were vivid yet foggy. The actions happened with sudden clarity, while the narrative was a dim visual that perhaps I could figure out, but likely not. There was a huge gothic house, not like mine, but old, really old. Dust flew from doorknobs, cobwebs shimmered in the stray strands of sun sneaking through cloth-eaten drapes. There was always a smell, a pungent smell of decay or cat piss. There was whispering, distant, just out of range of aural clarity. As I strained to hear the voices, in front of me a strange horror began to manifest. On the floor, on the carpet, in the dim of the night, a black mass rose. It was full of noises, deep growls and sounds that we laugh at in daylight as being Halloween sounds, but the reality is that they are frightening sounds in a dream.

I woke screaming and stared out at the room. Momentarily I forgot I was in Specimen 1's bed and was disoriented. A rush of coldness passed by me and I turned to see where the wind was coming from since the window was heavily barred and above my head. The many mirrors and toys reflected shards of light, a patchwork of mystery, waiting for me to unravel it. As I stared in awe around the room, my heart still pounding from my nightmare, the mass began to take shape at the foot of my bed. My heart began to race again as the mass rolled into itself, expanding wider and taller the longer I stared at it.

I blinked several times, hoping it was a trick of my eyes, but, no, there was something horrid rolling and growing. The room grew colder and I pulled the covers high over my head. I vaguely wondered if Specimen 1 had ever experienced that black mass while he lay there shackled. Poor guy, it likely drove him to madness to see that and not be able to do a thing about it.

I peeked out from my blankets but the room was still engulfed in blackness. A thick darkness that was deeper than the regular dimly lit room. Shadows didn't grow and hover and stay when there were no windows or lights to create them. A mass was forming around the bed. I squeezed my eyes tightly shut to block out the vision. I tried to focus on the terrible mess I would be facing in the attic in the morning and how I was going to be certain every drop of blood was gone for good.

Hands pulled back the covers. I screamed, but there was nothing there but the darkness enveloping me.

My electrodes were humming furiously. In this most terrifying of times, I was also craving my lovers. They were near. They were here.

As the black mass rolled and shifted around me, I saw fleeting glimpses of their faces. The beauty, the writer, the athlete, the musician. All laughing at me, enticing me, teasing me with unseen fingers, pulling at my nightgown, rubbing my flesh in the most glorious spots.

The room was darker as the pleasure built. The ghosts were all pleasuring me with their electrical energies. My body craved theirs, our patterns still working, their individual energies emerging briefly from the others and then diving back into the throng.

I cried with pleasure as our circuits danced and combined. My face was slick with sweat, my hands reaching out to unknown creatures, momentarily solid until slipping into ethereal nothingness again. A wave of growing ecstasy filled the room, the mass shifting and turning, my body filling and pulsing.

I came more times than I could count as the pleasure began to shift towards torment. I was exhausted. I needed to rest. Terror returned with the persistent clawing at my flesh. Streaks appeared, as if there really were fingernails scratching me.

I leaped from the bed and ran for the light switch. Obscured by the darkness of the mass, the light didn't illuminate the room one bit. I couldn't see who was tormenting me. My specimens. Demons.

I left Specimen 1's room and retired for the night in my own room, where the rest of the night proved to be uneventful.

*Journal*

The attic has been cleaned and preserved as best as I can manage. Specimen 1's room is now scrubbed and refreshed as well.

The musician's death was easy enough to deal with. But Specimen 1 was going to prove to be more difficult to cover up. I wasn't sure what to do. Part of me thought that I should have him found dead of a heart attack as he was and be done with it. However, the idea of keeping him alive appeals to me more. The experiment hasn't been completed yet so I can't report him missing.

Instead, I keep up his social media, which I'd always guarded anyway, and continued on as if he were alive and well and working on his novel.

I went through the manuscript. This second novel was nearly finished and there were extensive notes and chapter outlines, so it wouldn't be too hard to finish it up for him. I was a big enough fan to be able to emulate his style.

Of course, writing a novel is time consuming and boring. I discovered dictating the book while going about my business was working better for me. After I had all of that transcribed, I'd run it through a spinner that parroted the style of Scott Gravenhurst and it would be as if he'd written it himself.

The book wasn't due for a long time yet, so I wasn't worried about finishing it. I could likely do it in a weekend. I don't know what all the angst-ridden time wasting that writers experience is all about. A profession in the arts is one thing I can't wrap my head around.

So everything is as it should be.

Having no specimens at all is so freeing. I forgot how liberating it is to just be single. No one else to worry about. Just freedom.

But was I free?

I still had to keep an eye on the cadavers in the basement. Even if I didn't have to check daily, I still needed to keep on top on their vital signs. They have to remain at a specific range or there's no point in going through any of this. If the compounds aren't exact, they could rot, get brain damage, organ damage and so on. I wanted them to remain as wonderful as I could keep them, for as long as possible.

At night, I slept. Or tried to sleep. During the day, it was easy to push off the surreal rush of intrusive lust from four different lovers and give a lecture at the same time. I could pretend that twinges and tickles were menopause kicking in or the implants sparking. I knew what the sensations were, of course I did. The idea of it thrilled me and I kept careful track of the times and other important data in the other journal.

At night, however, they came to me. The black mass. The sudden chills. The endless orgasms. Night after night for nearly a week.

There is nothing I can do in the daylight hours to appease them. At this point, it's a timing thing. The various components need time to reprogram and regenerate. In the meantime electronic ghosts of my lovers come for me.

It was curious, how these lovers came to me, nearly always together. It was a side effect of the electromagnetic portion of the experiment. Between the serums and other factors, the implants still focus on their creator.


*Journal*

I am awakened in the night by a strange fluttering like butterfly wings and gentle, warm-fingered caresses along my body. Yet when I wake, there is nothing there.

*Journal*

They come for me at night, their tongues tasting, their fingers probing, their flesh rubbing around and in and through mine. I never know when they will arrive, circling me in a swirling mist, sparks of longing and lust palpitating from ethereal vapors. I can never ascertain how many of them there will be or who it will be that time. My specimens have come to play with me in their afterlife.

Specimen 1 often would make an appearance when I was watching television. His creative urgency pulsed frantically around me. Often the agitation was too much to bear and I learned that silencing him through the computer, by working on his book, was the best way to placate him.

Specimen 2 always appeared during my walks and the rare times I was allowed into the "exercise" room. If I was out in the yard and wandering with my thoughts, he would appear and urge me to go faster. Sometimes I ran in circles for long periods of time. I don't know how far or how long, I lost track of time when I channeled him. At least he let me go to the gym too for my classes, which kept me in the public eye and kept me from going too mad.

Specimen 3 was in the mirror. As narcissistic as I'd always been, suddenly I was catapulted to a whole new level. My makeup changed dramatically to that of a high-fashion model with the latest season's colors splashed in slashes along my eyes and high cheekbones. I wore my hair in a brunette, shoulder-length, layered cut with streaks of red. Suddenly every blemish on my face was a big concern and I spend many a time on the exercise bike with some kind of mask on my face.

Their nightly visits had now penetrated my days.

*Specimen 4*

I turned off his devices permanently. His charms were removed from my bracelet. His essence is no more. His exit relieves me a tiny bit. One less specimen to juggle.

*Journal*

I took to my bed with nervous exhaustion.

Truly, I collapsed one day, coming in through the door. I couldn't go on. Suddenly, my legs stopped working and I plunged to the floor.

As I lay there, I realized I could sleep for a year. Finally, I gathered my wits together and began a slow crawl up the stairs towards my room. The buzzing and frantic urgency of the specimens raced through my body, each nerve its own pathway up and down my spine until my brain wanted to scream.

I took to my bed to calm my nerves. There had been too much going on. It was time to get a grip.

The day before I had spent the afternoon creating a new recording. This one would hopefully make the bedroom my cone of silence for a few hours before their electrodes homed in on me again. I turned down all the devices on my bracelet, even though I was always turning them down. Yet they would always creep back up again. I couldn't turn the charms off completely or the specimens would disappear forever and the point of the experiment would be lost.

As I turned down the charms for Specimen 1, I realized how much I missed him. I miss taking him to my university events and going to the pubs. I missed him reading to me at night.

If there was ever a time I wish I could re-create, it would be that first time we met, loving each other in the staff bathroom. The naughtiness, his beauty, the anticipation of everything that lay before me at that time, the unknown—it was all wrapped up in that moment. That was the moment I wanted back.

I had re-created it. And it had worked. For a moment. In the moment. Then it fell away once more.

I drank wine and wept, watching *West Side Story* and then *Sweeney Todd*. When the movies ended and I had cried my fill, I went to the bathroom.

When I looked in the mirror, I saw the face of my own insanity staring back at me. I stared at the brown patches under my eyes, my hollow grey cheeks, my saggy skin. My hair was sticking out all crazy, like an Amanda Palmer rag doll.

I ran to my bedroom vanity and sat down in the little chair, staring into the makeup mirror.

I stared like a zombie. My beautiful looks were ravaged by my experiments. What is the price of finding the ultimate pleasure? I had opened Pandora's box—no, worse, that *Hellraiser* box—and now I was paying the price for my pleasure with my beauty.

As I sobbed anew, my head on my arms, soothing hands stroked my shoulders. Specimen 3 guided me with stern and gentle hands to make myself beautiful once more. Sure, my makeup was a disaster after my days of bed-ridden angst but I could brush my teeth and comb my hair, hell, even remember to wash it once in a while. I could do that and did.

The other specimens slipped through the cracks in the sound. I knew my cone of silence wouldn't last, and soon they were around me once more. I turned off the recording as their electronic touches brought me back to life and back to ecstasy.

*Journal*

The lack of flesh and bone made their pleasures even more exquisite. I wondered what it would be like when I had no more flesh and bone. Would their pleasures be magnified? Or would I not feel them anymore?

*Journal*

They've consumed me, created me to be all of them.

I rise at six every morning to run several miles before I sit down at the computer to write. Around ten o'clock I take a long, leisurely shower and groom myself to perfection before sitting back down at the computer. At three o'clock I ride my bike for about five miles around a local park and when I return I shower and groom again. Then I eat like a pig, have a few drinks, watch TV, then write some more until I collapse from exhaustion—and do it all over again the next day.

I've been writing as Specimen 1—he controls the keyboard as the words click onto the screen.

I actually placed tenth in a triathlon. It was really a baby triathlon but I never thought I'd do anything like that in my life.

When I won my latest award for research in electroneurological research, a national magazine decided they wanted to do an entire photo spread on me, the sexy scientist.

However, somewhere inside of me, my physical body is tired again.

Sometimes I wish I could have my specimens all go away until the next part of the experiment can begin.

Not unless I have some sort of major electrical shift.

If I myself did something different electronically, perhaps. But I'm not sure. I would hate to alter my circuits only to find that when I'm ready to reprogram there is a flaw in the data, although there should only be perfection in my many sets of notes.

All I can do is wait. Waiting is difficult in these times but there's nothing else to be done.

*Journal*

They are with me always and I'm sure I look half-mad out in public. They tease and torment me as I run my errands, and I beg them to leave me alone.

Though, I must admit, I do enjoy the constant state of arousal. That constant quiver that never ends. Each orgasm fills and empties me with tremendous waves of pleasure and melancholy.

However, even someone as lusty as me has a limit. Pleasure, perfection, has done its time. My search for perfection must continue.

No matter how I adjust the frequencies, they do not leave me. I tried the cone of silence idea once more but it failed miserably. I had barely pressed Play on the recording when they were back, tickling my hair, stroking my thighs, invading my thoughts with their own wants and needs.

Yet each one of them mirrors all of mine perfectly.

I'm in perfection overdrive.

*Specimen 5*

It was a spontaneous decision to add Specimen 5 to the mix. There was something about her that I needed to have, that I craved to be part of my life. Something familiar about her, an echo from a haunted dream, fueled my obsession even though I had already decided that the three muses were all that I needed.

I didn't have to find her at the sex club. She appeared in my dancercise class. A buxom, slender woman who wore tight spandex T-backs and bicycle shorts that highlighted her perfect apple-cheeked ass. I was in love the moment I cast eyes upon her.

For several weeks I'd noticed her in the class, watched her jump around behind me reflected in the mirror, gazed adoringly at the sweat that dribbled from her forehead.

In the showers after class, I hoped to speak with her one day.

That day came mere hours ago.

She was showering in the stall next to me. My heart beat rapidly as I listened to her shampoo her hair, humming softly. I heard the shower turn off and I in turn did the same. We both stepped out naked at the same time, reaching for our towels. My eyes beheld the gloriousness of her firm young body, her high breasts, the soft folds of barely touched flesh between her legs.

"Hello," I said as I wrapped my towel around my waist, walking from the stall to the locker room. She walked with me, towel slung across her shoulders.

"Hi," she said.

"My name's Miriam," I said, holding out my hand.

"Cindy," she said.

As we arrived at the locker room, we realized our lockers were in the same alcove. She began to speak nervously, as if I were going to do something to her. It was rather odd.

"I'm a student, studying neurology. I know your work." She smiled. She seemed eager for my response as she perched like a puppy, hands clasped in anticipation of a positive answer.

"Do tell, which work would that be? I'm involved in several projects."

"All of it, I think, I hope. I've been kind of a fan of yours for years. I'd been hoping to one day get a chance to talk to you."

She pulled on her T-shirt and smiled over at me. She kept trying to explain herself.

"Underground research fascinates me the most. You know, reanimating corpses, just like Frankenstein."

"Well, we've come a long way in science, but there's still a long way more to go. Reanimating body parts is old hat these days. Playing puppet master to dead chunks of flesh is really just a matter of stimulating the proper points, oxygen, blood flow…"

"Oh, I know that. I like the ideas about brainwashing and creating lifemates. Those are the studies I find most fascinating."

"I find most people I meet want to talk about those ideas most of all," I said.

"Will you teach me? Will you let me come study with you, at least for a while, or even once. One hour. Just to let me see how it's done. How the master works and plays," she said as she pulled on her jeans.

"Let me think about it," I said with a smile. A sudden headache pierced my temples. I raised my hands in pain.

"Oh." The word slipped out unexpectedly.

"Something wrong, Dr. Frederick?" she asked me, snapping her jeans.

"No, just a sudden headache. Probably a workout headache or something…too long in the shower." I muttered excuses and willed the headache to leave me. My finger buzzed as I shut the locker door, a mild electrical shock surged through me. I pulled away and there was a small arc. Specimen 5 saw me jump back.

"Are you all right, Doctor? Do you need to sit down?" She stepped towards me and I stepped back.

"No, I'm good. It's all good," I said.

I wondered if one of my implants had malfunctioned. It was not outside the realm of possibility. The headache pulsed and I went into the toilet stall and sat down. I rubbed my temples as I urinated. The headache wasn't a regular stress headache or an allergy headache. It was a buzzing, annoying headache and I knew it was because of at least one of the specimens.

After splashing water on my face, I looked at myself in the mirror. I had to pull myself together. The headache caused me to see glimpses of bright lights shimmering out of the corners of my eyes.

My face appeared normal in the reflection, business as usual, yet the inner turmoil hurtling through my brain raged on.

The headache began to throb with more persistence. In fact, it rippled along from one temple to the other, sometimes around the back of my head, sometimes around the top. I returned to the locker room to find Specimen 5 fully dressed. She handed me a business card.

"Call me when you want me to start," she said.

"I haven't agreed to see you at all yet," I said as I made a valiant attempt not to stagger under the vertigo of the headache.

"However much time you can give me, I'm yours." She smiled and left the locker room. I heard her boots clicking down the hallway and out the door.

In that moment, my headache was too overwhelming to do much more than get dressed and get out. As I drove home, I decided that I would indeed tutor her in neurological sciences for a while.

*Journal*

My four specimens don't like Specimen 5 at all. They are more annoying than ever when they swarm around me. I wonder if she thinks I suffer from a tic, or if she can see or sense their electrical charges snapping and swimming through the air. I wonder how I really look to others as I try to ignore the niggling pests.

She has been coming over to learn from me for several days now. I'm high on her thirst for knowledge, adore her pale face and worship her perfect, lean body. Her dark eyes gaze at me with such intensity that I often wanted to kiss her.

I did lean over to kiss her last night. She was watching me with those eyes, those delicious chocolate eyes, and my mouth watered. I licked my lips and pursed them.

I leaned forward to kiss her. Just as her lips were about to touch mine, there was a spark between us. Specimen 5 lurched back on the chair, her hand to her mouth.

"What was that?" she cried out. The smell of singed flesh wafted by for a moment and was gone.

"It must have been carpet shock," I said. "I'm so sorry."

She gave me a look as if she didn't believe me. I knew I wasn't sounding convincing as I touched my own lips and tasted Specimen 3's perfume.

I didn't try to kiss her again. She placed her delicate, pale hand on my lap. I shivered as she touched me, answering her never-ending supply of questions about my work. She was hungry for my knowledge and I was thrilled to have an eager student willing to listen to my theories and rants.

Sometimes when she was listening, she would quickly pull her hand from me, as if she had been slapped. I'd keep talking but wondered if it were possible for the electromagnetic fields programmed for me to jump to her briefly since my focus was on her?

Her hand traveled along my leg and she leaned forward as if to kiss me. I leaned towards her and an arc of electricity surged between us. We both jumped back and held our mouths with our hands. After a moment, Specimen 5 lowered her hands. She stared at me as if waiting for an answer. I said nothing.

"Well, I'd say it's time to call it a day…whatever's going on," Specimen 5 said, gathering up her notes and books. She kept a safe distance from me and hurried towards the door.

"Will I see you at the gym?" I asked her, my interest in her returning as my lips ached from the shocking almost kiss.

"I'm sure you will, thank you for your help," she said. She couldn't get out of my house fast enough.

As I locked the door after her I yelled to the air.

"Stop bothering her. I'm allowed to do whatever I want."

I wondered if they were ghosts or just electricity. What was making them sabotage my time with Specimen 5 but not with anyone else ever, even among each other?

Was it just a part of their loyalty programming to keep me from her? But it didn't make sense. The continuity wasn't there.

Sadly, I watched her walk down the porch stairs, wondering if I dared to do what I dreamed.

*Journal*

Whenever I see her, they are angry. They twist and spark around me. I can smell my flesh burning as they snap their displeasure.

I can't even program the iPod for her; they continue to interfere with my settings, short-circuiting any electronic manipulation I might try.

It still isn't time to continue on to the next phase. I have to think of something to keep them at bay.

*Journal*

I sat in the writer's chair, my fingers perched on his keyboard as I waited for him to channel through me for that day's notes and journals, and, of course, a page or two for his book.

I poured his favorite scotch (undrugged) into a glass filled with ice and took a small sip. I took a drag from his favorite cigarette. I thought about the year or so he sat in this chair. How much I adored watching him work, staring at his strong, firm fingers punching the wireless keyboard as I dreamed of them touching me.

And how now he never stops.

I conducted some calculations since my last entry and determined that I may be able to block all of their frequencies for a short time. I would have to work fast because I didn't want them to disappear forever either.

A few hours ago, I finally, reluctantly, sadly, roughly, quickly, removed all my implants. It was depressing and painful work to dig out the little electrodes from my genitals and breasts and head. I'll have some nasty wounds for a while. I didn't have the time or patience to go slowly and carefully. They were still turned on and so were the ghosts. Now they are with me in my pocket.

I scooped the implants out of my pocket and placed the tiny metal pellets on Specimen 1's keyboard. I watched as his essence buzzed along with the exposed electrodes. I had rigged a small handset to program the electrodes, as they wouldn't respond to my brain impulses and pheromones anymore. I turned the dials slightly and punched in a digital code. More essence swam forth and I knew it was Specimen 2. I could tell it was him because I suddenly wanted to abandon my experiment and go run on the treadmill.

At last, I had the two of them swarming along the keyboard. I couldn't quite see or feel them, but I knew they were there, feasting on each other, transparent electromagnetic waves winding and weaving through each other like ribbons on a Maypole.

I put the keyboard and the specimens into a big demagnetized bag. I carried it carefully up the stairs to my newest laboratory, a hidden one behind the walls where the walk-in pantry and a little bathroom used to be. Beyond that, there was what looked like another large room from the outside of the house, with a false wall of drapes and plants.

Inside was a plush gothic bedroom where Specimen 3 resided. Black metal and ruby-red velvet were the accents around the room. Of course, half the room was the necessary surgical bed, lamps and other equipment that kept her alive.

I had revived her a week or so ago. Her reanimation is recorded in another journal that has all the specifics of every formula and preparation. Needless to say, scientists have been able to reanimate corpses for decades; they just don't want the public to know.

It was not the most pleasant task, taking her out of the tank. She wasn't the specimen I wanted to reanimate first. All the plans were for Specimen 1 and it wasn't time yet. But I was going mad with the rebellion of the implants and needed to take action.

It took her a few days to grow used to breathing and walking and all of those normal tasks. She was allowed to wander around the room unhindered since she mostly just sat and posed. Until she was more viable, she was no threat.

It seemed best to keep her on an upper level where I could access her more easily. Her rebirth wasn't pleasant, it was very premature, and she was still very delicate.

Specimen 3 has been rather stunned at her new surroundings. I do suspect some brain damage but she is still so very beautiful, despite issues with her decaying flesh. She looked sallow, her usual milk-chocolate-colored glow tinged yellow. Perhaps from daylight. Perhaps from rigor mortis setting in. Maybe I had miscalculated the preservation formulas. How I hoped not, or I'd be stuck reassessing the problem again.

"Hello," I said to her as she sat on the black velvet fainting couch. I kissed her briefly on her cold, damp cheek. She said nothing, just stared like a doll.

"Come over here and lie down," I instructed as I led her over to the metal operating table. She lay down and I raised the bed higher. She whimpered a little bit, almost holding her breath as the table raised.

"This won't take long," I said as I wheeled over the tray of tools. I brought the bag with the keyboard and my implants. She lay patiently, crying out a little when my sharp sterilized scalpel nicked a tiny incision to slip new implants into her.

Several nicks around her body later, she was done. I closed up each little incision with a staple, in case she had any thoughts about digging them out with those long claws of hers. But then again, she probably doesn't even have the reasoning skills left to think about digging them out. Still, the staples would secure the implants, even in her clitoris.

Once she was finished, I put headphones on her and played some Linkin Park/Jay-Z *Collision Course* for her. She watched me with those pretty green eyes. Well, they weren't so pretty and green anymore. They had a milky film over them, much like cataracts. I would have to get my beauty some colored contact lenses.

I went over to the bag and brought it back to her. I smiled as I opened it and could almost see my men zip out in joy and home in on her newest implants. I put my own implants into a tiny vial. I would be needing them again very soon, once Specimen 1 was ready for the next phase.

As Specimen 3 lay strapped to the table, the ghosts sending her into ecstasy, I breathed a sigh of relief. For the first time in nearly two years, I was free of each and every one of them. I'd forgotten what it was like, to not feel them constantly with me.

Her moans and sighs filled the room and I turned away, bittersweet, as my specimens all played together.

But now I was free at last to explore the final Specimen. Number 5. I could take my time to decide what her future would include. And this time I won't be swept away by idle folly.

*Specimen 1*

Late at night, I creep down to the lab where his body floats in preparation. I bring with me a book of poetry and a bottle of wine. He is still very handsome as he floats in his tank. I'm filled with excitement at how we'll be together again, just he and I, as it should have always been.

I'll drink the wine and read the poetry to him, dreaming of the future when he will wrap his arms around me once more and speak to me with that wonderful voice. How we will talk of all the strange ideas in life, how we will watch the sunsets, how I will take him on trips to places he's only dreamed about. I dream of a marvelous future for Specimen 1 and me.

If the calculations work out correctly, if the flesh can withstand the process, if the electrodes will function correctly when all placed together in one perfect container…so many ifs for my perfect future with the man who I realize now is my perfect mate.

*Specimen 5*

Yet while time needs to pass, I could never be bored with someone who had a mind as brilliant as mine. I would be her mentor and teach her everything. I can groom her to follow in my footsteps and encourage her to the greatest of heights. Every day would be a new mountain to climb as we spurred her on to the top.

*Specimen 5 (written on torn up scraps of paper)*

Well, that didn't go as planned. I didn't second-guess her own pathological nature.

I am in a cage. A foul-smelling, cement-floor, basement cage in some horribly dank house somewhere.

I don't know where. I presume I'm in a city because I hear rumblings on a pretty regular basis that might be streetcars or subways.

*(scrap)*

There is an air bed, yes, and I pray the rats don't gnaw through it one day, but they will.

The other day I felt one run up my leg, under my covers, in the middle of the night.

*(scrap)*

I am locked like a rat in a cage and yet the rats willingly join me. It's rather hilarious. Kind of like that Smashing Pumpkins song.

Anyway, before I go completely mad from the drugs she slips me, though I try to avoid what I can detect by spitting it out or holding it til she's gone, I need to make notes, no matter how illegible they may become.

*(scrap)*

My body shivers and jitters, she has put implants in me, but they are not soft and calming. They hurt like a bitch and no matter what throes of arousal I may achieve; the pain is excruciating.

*(scrap)*

My head aches as she flips around my brain waves through her computer just outside of my cage and even from her cell phone when she leaves me. I know it's her. I can feel the switches being turned on and off.

I wonder if my specimens ever felt them, my manipulations in their brains. I always wanted to ask, but never did. I didn't want them to know that I knew something was "wrong". Instead, I wanted them to believe they were going crazy.

And now I'm the one going crazy.

And despite going crazy, one thing I know: the specimen never gets returned to its former life.

*(scrap)*

I should have known not to trust her, back when she asked me why I hadn't conducted experiments in the past five years. My studies had abruptly stopped, yet I continued to get grants.

I didn't answer her directly, of course, I just fudged some babble and she passively took it.

But that should have been the first red flag that the hunter was being hunted.

*(scrap)*

The weeks that have passed, it's been hell. I'm surprised I can hold a pen or even formulate coherent thoughts at all.

*Journal*

At last I've regained control of my journal through a series of events that will be explained.

For many days, she had me shackled to a wall, spread-eagled and naked. Now and again I'd be turned over to be flogged, tenderized for the feast. I was in pain where there were pussing, gaping gashes that marked the incisions for her clumsy implants. I had so many of them too. I couldn't figure out what theory or method she might be using for her choices.

"What do you want from me?" I'd cry out to her, but she'd never answer, just whip me harder. I was being punished, but I didn't know my crime.

At times I wondered—was she following the model for perfection?

Throughout it all, she herself was still perfection. Who couldn't admire the brilliance of such a scholar, a real Svengali and a genius with theories that might be proving true? Her body was pure poetry, her eyes hypnotic; anyone would do what she'd ask. I did.

The days and nights melted together in agonizing slowness, yet I still had no concept of how long I was there. She humiliated me in every way imaginable, demanding that I urinate and defecate into a bucket and flogging me if I dared say a word. She pulled my hair, kissing me, and mocking me, and I cast my eyes down, trembling under the touch of this beautiful mistress.

She'd get into moods where she'd sexually arouse me. Licking and fondling and using an assortment of toys on my body. I was helpless under her touch, her beauty mocking her evil as she led me into orgasm after orgasm.

And each time I felt something shift in my brain. Turn the channel. Surf a frequency.

I guess she grew bored of me at some point. I'm not sure what experiment she was conducting at that time—maybe pleasure and pain, and need and orgasm? At any rate, one day I was ordered back into my cage and that's where I stayed for a very long time.

That time I wasn't alone in the cage.

In my absence, she had brought in Specimen 3. Poor Specimen 3. She was truly falling apart. No mud baths would help that sad, sorry face now. It was pretty much sliding off her skull and the stink of her rotting flesh overwhelmed the room. I wasn't much better off, with my weeping, infected sores, along with the scars from the whip.

Specimen 3 had been glad to see me. Oh how she had missed me. She threw her arms around me, trying to kiss me with those foul swollen lips. I pushed her away, knowing it was in vain if the new implants worked at all.

It was hellish. Eventually it was easier to succumb to her desires than to lead her on a rotting, fetid, exhausting chase around the room, especially when technology was in charge. The implants buzzed and clicked, and it saddened me that Specimen 5 had used such primitive technology when so much better stuff was available.

And how can you kill something that is already dead? Specimen 3 was not really Beauty anymore, just a walking infected pus bag with electrodes. Even if the body was gone, the electrodes lived on.

So I let the creature "live" and feast as she wished on her desires.

I patted her head, my hand trembling as I stroked her hair, but not from desire.

"It's okay," I'd reassure Specimen 3. She grunted and pushed her face against mine. The smell was too close and my stomach lurched. Sourness filled the back of my throat but I swallowed down the bile. She kissed me, her swollen, broken fingers rummaging between my legs until they filled my pussy. The electrodes stimulated me, but the vileness of the smells and textures made me wish for anything but sex with this creature.

However, she was unrelenting. Every day. All day. Pushing her fingers into me, smashing her face to mine or to my crotch. Sensations so dreadfully unpleasant, yet still filling me up and satisfying my cravings.

Specimen 5 was right there, watching this vile creation defile me, writing notes in her notebook while she grinned.

*Journal*

I found out more—why she was observing me and Specimen 3 together. Why she kept reprogramming the lust higher and the cravings for me deeper when it was clear that Specimen 3 was not much more than a rotting corpse.

Specimen 5 loved making Specimen 3 want to love me all the time. It gave her great joy, a bit of a respite, and sort of revenge.

For what was likely the thousandth time, I called out from my cage, "What do you want from me?"

And for the first time ever, she put down her pen and answered me, "Do you remember Leonard Penny?" she asked me in a soft voice. It took me a while to go back in my brain.

"Leonard Penny…"

"Yes, Leonard Penny," she said. "Do you remember him at all?"

I sighed. Yes, I did.

"He was my brother," she said coldly.

It turned out that Specimen 5 was the little sister of Specimen C6. I conducted a round of experiments in the early 2000s and her brother was one of the guinea pigs. I did remember C6 fondly, as I do all my specimens. I always pick them for a reason. It's so odd how human nature lets the lust and love wear off, no matter how perfect something is. I can only be grateful that I didn't use electrodes back then, more of a concoction of chemicals that might trigger pheromones and such. So primitive. Anyway, C6 was a tall, thin art student at the local college. I had seven specimens over the course of that set.

"Your brother," I said.

"Yes, you used my brother as one of your experiments. I remember how excited he'd been the day he'd signed up for an experiment from a note posted on a campus board. I was just a kid back then. I barely knew what science was, let alone experiments. And, certainly, I would never have guessed what would happen to my big brother."

"I don't believe your brother was in my experiment," I lied.

"Oh yes, he was. He described you so perfectly. He was a student in one of your classes. He went to sign up for the top-secret experiment. And then...one day...he just disappeared. Just like that. Gone."

She sighed and looked at me. I said nothing. I let no emotion cross my face. She couldn't prove anything at all.

"I've been following you for years. Only in the past couple of years did I come to realize what it is you do and how you destroy other people to satisfy your own lusty cravings."

"Oh please...scientists have to conduct experiments. You know that. And I had nothing to do with your brother's disappearance."

"Ah, but you did. I've explored and dug through your life, your files, your computers. I've had PIs on your ass for years. I know more about you and your motives than you likely do."

"Don't kid yourself," I said, pacing in my cage. I wish she would burn some incense or spray some air freshener around, but she never did. She enjoyed me living in the filthy stench of the cage with my bloated, maggot-infested roommate. She enjoyed waving a vanilla-scented handkerchief in front of her own nose every few minutes.

"Your lust is your downfall. Why couldn't you just be happy fucking all your friends and be done with it?"

"There's so much more…"

"No, there isn't. You keep trying to discover a soul mate, soul-mate connections, lust connections, love, dependency… It doesn't exist. Don't you see? You keep chasing an illusion, which is why you always fail."

I thought about Specimen 1. What would have happened if we'd just dated like normal people?

Well, nothing, really. He'd have left me that first weekend to go back to his girlfriend and it would have ended there. The nights of wine and poetry, of orgies and sex clubs, none of it would have ever happened at all.

"You can't make someone love you, Doctor." Specimen 5 laughed at me.

"I didn't want anyone to love me."

"You wanted full, unconditional love from the perfect mate with qualities of brains, beauty and strength. And what have you now? Your Beauty is right there… You ruined her yourself, but she still loves you. Yet now you don't love her."

I had no answer.

"What is the purpose of your experiments, except to fulfill your own narcissistic lust?" she asked me.

"I'm solving the puzzle of the human mind, how we act and react in lust and love."

"And my brother?"

"Your brother isn't here," I said.

"No, he's not anywhere. I looked through your house and he was nowhere. Just a number in a journal somewhere, I'm sure. An experiment…and that was all he was to you. Not human, just a cock."

"Each one of my specimens had a purpose."

"To feed your massive ego and your sexual perversions."

I laughed in her face.

"My ego rides waves like everyone else's. And I'm not alone. So many people have no interpersonal skills. So many people use others for horrible reasons, and sex is certainly one of them. I would suggest that nearly everyone uses everyone else for some form of sexual desire and comfort, even if it isn't consummated."

She let me continue by being silent.

"Who doesn't like that heady lust of infatuation, the adrenaline rush from the thrill of the hunt, the conquest? Who doesn't love that wonderful first fuck and that amazing first orgasm when everything is perfect? Why not capture it and live it forever?"

She stood up and left the room.

My only flaw was not accounting for human nature to grow bored. Disinterest. Apathy. Dissent. I thought I had picked truly perfect specimens, and I had. But the thrill of the hunt dissipated within me. No matter what they did, they couldn't please me.

The ADD of lust.

No matter how I had tampered with the codes, I couldn't get past the basic human instinct of the predator. And if there's no hunting, there's no motivation, no thrill of the chase.


Specimen 5 never ventured into the cage. She wore big netted hats and covered herself from head to toe, in white, including little white cotton gloves. No lab coats for her. She was all frills and layers. Her eyes gleamed from behind her glasses through the net. I feel like I'm in some bizarre movie in a foreign land. Even *Midnight Express* wasn't this bad. The volume of bugs in my prison, courtesy of rotting Beauty, was disgusting. Flies and maggots, cockroaches and giant water beetles. Millipedes and, I don't doubt, bedbugs. Because of the itching and scratching, my body looked nearly as bad as Specimen 3's .

When I see Specimen 5 in her wide-brimmed hat, I'm reminded of Jessica Lange in *All That Jazz*. Lange played the role of Death. There were many times that I figured I was going to die under the hands of Specimen 5 if I couldn't outwit her. As for the Death outfit, she was protecting herself from all the bugs.

There was no protection for me.


One day, my luck changed.

Specimen 5 took me from the bedroom where I had been kept. I pretended to be drugged and ill when, in fact, I'd managed for three days in a row to avoid taking the drug. Little did she know that I spent a lot of time doing push-ups and planks and practicing my kickboxing and even jogging in place whenever I was free from her shackles.

She stopped to unlock the door and I clocked her good. She fell down and I stomped on her beautiful face. Hard. She cried out some kind of unearthly yelp and I stomped on her windpipe as well. I kicked her several times until she was just a bloody, pulpy mess. No more beautiful face for her. Or brilliant schemes to destroy me.

I ran up the stairs and went into the main floor of the house. It was a bungalow and I found the bathroom readily. I paused and looked in the mirror. I couldn't go out looking like that. Plus, there was a body or two in the basement. I had to pull myself together in the event anyone spotted me. I quickly took a shower, reveling in how wonderful it was to use soap and wash my hair.

I dug at my genitals and the rest of my body to dig out her implants. It was harder than when I did it to myself because they were larger and I had no scalpel. I broke a razor apart and used the blade to part reluctant skin.

She had so many of them in me I didn't even know if I'd find them all. At last, bloodied and raw, I emerged from the shower and wiped myself down with all the towels I could find.

I found clothes to wear in the closet and got out as fast as I could. I was tempted to take her car, but instead just grabbed a couple hundred bucks from her wallet and tried to figure out where I was and where I was going.

However, I didn't worry too much since she was lying dead in the basement, no doubt with Specimen 3's reanimated corpse cradling her.


*Journal*

I returned to my home. I didn't know what I would find there. I wasn't pleased with what was left. The first place I went was down to the back laboratory to check on Specimen 1 in his tank.

He was gone.

She had taken him away.

Seeing the empty tank was a stab to my heart.

She had destroyed my experiment.

She had destroyed Specimen 1.

The overwhelming shock of knowing I'd never see Specimen 1 again filled me with rage and grief. At first, I could only scream, throwing whatever was near me and smashing it on the ground.

When my rage subsided, I collapsed in grief. My sobs echoed through the empty room, a reminder of how alone I truly was.

*Journal*

I woke in the night to a horrific sight. They were there. All of them. Specimen 1 with glowing blue eyes. The pale-green, pussy, infection-ridden hands of Specimen 3 reaching for me, tugging my bedclothes from me as I slept. Specimen 2 a shimmer, electrical energy circling me. It didn't matter that I had no implants. My specimens knew me and reached out for me.

There is nothing I can do now, I'm too exhausted and must heal. I'll let them play with me until I can figure it out. After all, they know all my pleasure zones, so why hurry?

I drifted back to sleep as my phantoms haunted me.

*Journal*

So if I have no implants, why are they still there? The pheromones and the brain waves perhaps?

They are energy.

Or were they just dreams?

*Journal*

Life went on for quite some time. I conducted theoretical research on what my next project might be.

There was nothing that really came to mind. I wasn't sure how much further I could go with the idea of perfection without somehow removing the component of apathy, complacency, being taken for granted or whatever it is. But even if I could somehow do it, it would be too complex to program the specimens and myself to not have those human components.

I went to the clubs and the gym and walked by the lake and went shopping and even attended parties with my colleagues. They re-embraced me, at the usual arm's length, and I could see in their eyes that I had changed somehow, and I'm sure I have.

I often thought about Specimen 1 and wondered where she had put him. He must still be at the bungalow, but I couldn't return to the scene of the crime. Although his essence comes to me, I miss him. I miss our conversations. I miss watching him write his book.

*Journal*

In the night, I felt him. Different this time. I was startled awake in the darkness by the sense of someone standing over me. Yet this time it was not a ghost, an apparition, a rainbow, a vibration, an orb. No, it was him. Specimen 1. His shadow was outlined in the glow from the streetlamps leaking through the curtains.

"Scott?" I sat up. His eyes glowed blue in the darkness.

"Miriam," he said coldly, the word thick in his lips.

"You came back?" I asked. "Why?"

"Where else can I go like this?"

He fell onto my bed, his body cold. I pulled the covers over him. It was dark so I couldn't see him, but he didn't smell very good. I figured he'd likely been sleeping in alleys and dumpsters. In the morning, I would help him wash and get back to normal.

"Miriam, is it you?" he asked, reaching his hands out to clutch at my arms. Instead of his familiar firm grip, his fingers were soft. The sensation was like a pair of soft beanbags enveloping my arms.

"Yes," I said, my eyes adjusting to the dimness.

His eyes reflected the light, glowing as he examined my face.

"I can't believe I found you again," he said. I wrapped my arms around him but recoiled at his texture. I lurched back and turned on the bedside lamp. He was hideous in his appearance.

His flesh was bloated, split open in many places where wounds pussed out. He was dripping all over my bedding.

"Scott... Let's get you in the shower," I said as I silently cursed Specimen 5. How dare she animate him before he was ready? He would have been perfect had she left him alone.

I led him to the shower, trying not to gag at his smell.

"Step into the stall but don't turn it on,.I'll be right back," I said as I grabbed the air freshener that was on the bathroom counter and sprayed it around the room.

I hurried to the upstairs lab and found several spools of bandages, alcohol and bags full of other equipment, and brought them to the bathroom. I took some sponges from under the sink.

It was a long, slow process to sponge down the worst of the wounds. It seemed that rigor mortis was seeping through him, yet he still lived. Parts of him were still vital, such as his strong, firm legs that didn't seem to have anything wrong with them at all. However, from his waist up there was a severe problem. It appeared as if he'd been sitting half-in, half-out of a freezer for six months and then defrosted, although that wasn't the reality either. His face had a mottled green-and-blue pallor, his lips rotted and black, his gums blackened where several teeth had fallen out. His arms were the worst, with splitting skin from his wrist, across his shoulders and along his back. Small nests of maggots squirmed in many of the cracks.

Swallowing down the urge to vomit, I steeled myself into doctor mode. I took his blood pressure, listened to his heart, and made all the necessary documentation about his vital signs.

With a scalpel, and donning a mask and gloves, of course, I set about digging out the pockets of fly eggs from his wounds. He grimaced, but it was more of a reflex than from any pain, I'm quite certain. However, there was no denying the foul pungent smell of death that loomed in the room.

I continued cleansing the wounds and patting them dry. Then began the task of wrapping him. It took a long time, but in the end, he was wrapped from the top of his head to his waist. It was my hope that the antibiotic-laden gauze would hold him together while I considered how to save him. Should I fill him with more fluids through IV or would it be a pointless exercise? I wasn't certain any of the equipment even worked; she had gone through my entire house, trashing some items, not trashing others.

Specimen 1 was silent throughout the ministrations.

There were so many questions I wanted to ask him but, instead, I let him keep his silence.

It was better just to try to get some sleep. We went to his apartment since my bed wasn't fit for sleeping and it was already nearing dawn. He walked slowly, wearing briefs on his freshly hand-showered lower body. He walked with a limp and was an odd sight, looking like the invisible man from the waist up.

"How do you always manage to get into my room?" I asked him. "It's always bothered me, wondering how you did that?"

"Where there's a will, there's a way," he said.

"I've watched you in the cameras and I don't understand."

"It doesn't matter," he said. "Why do you think I'd ever tell you as long as I'm still alive."

"You're not alive, Scott," I said. "Sorry."

"Of course I am. I'm thinking original thoughts. I'm not a computer program."

"As long as the battery holds out," I muttered.

We slept together in his bed, his smell tamed with the perfumes of modern times coupled with the menthol aroma of the medicine. We lay together in the bed, both on our backs, his bandaged hand lightly holding mine. He fell asleep quickly. I was surprised that he would need to sleep. It's hard to determine how to classify him.

Just as I was drifting off to sleep, that twilight slumber where you're just about to tumble off the reality cliff and into the dreamscape, the room grew cold. I squinted open my eyes and immediately looked towards the window to see if someone had come into the room.

There was no one there, yet I felt like I was being watched. The black mass began to grow and rise at the foot of the bed. I didn't say anything to Specimen 1. I just watched in awe as the mass tumbled forth. It hovered over the bed, looming and expanding, a heavy blackness that enveloped both me and Specimen 1. I shut my eyes and didn't open them again until I felt the warm rays of dawn on my eyelids.

I lay staring at the sun coming in through the window, the creature quiet beside me. I pondered the various ways to reanimate him, but none was viable with the rotting flesh. There may be a way to patch the rot with fresh flesh. There may be a way to switch body parts, but for that there needed to be access to healthy people, healthy flesh. I didn't have that access.

As I mused, hoping to discover a hole in the problem that I hadn't quite seen yet, Specimen 1 flung his bandaged arm across me, hugging me to him in a spoon. His body flush against mine, he was hard in his dreams. I wiggled back against him, angling myself so that his still-perfect cock entered me. I nearly cried with relief, with desire, as we moved together in a sleepy morning rhythm. His cock sliding in and out of me was a blessing I never thought I'd experience in the flesh again. I let myself enjoy his thrusts, enjoying the sideways lovemaking. My fingers played with myself as he rocked me, and I indulged myself wholeheartedly with a climax, and then two.

When he came, the sounds that came from him were unearthly. A howl like a dying animal. He trembled and held me to him; then he sobbed. I didn't once look at him, wanting to remember the vibrant young writer I'd met at the university.

At last, I released myself from his hold. I crawled from the bed, now a soupy mess from his infections, loosened bandages and our sweat.

In the shower, I cried and part of me wished he would be gone when I returned back to the bedroom. After all, there were no more locks, no more chastity belts, no more bracelet.

But he was there, sitting up, his bandaged hands holding his bandaged head.

"Help me," he whispered.

*Specimen 1*

He was real. He was alive. My shock and joy at seeing him made flesh once more was a combination of awe and fear.

He was not doing well. His body was falling apart. And his handsome face wasn't handsome at all. Blue-green, bloated, swollen, flesh actually ripped and torn in spots like old clothes.

"How did you…get like this?" I asked him.

"I don't know. I remember some woman doing things to me in the lab. Cutting, poking, prodding. She took me somewhere else. But then she just never came back. I was able to escape and found my way back here. You have to help me, Doctor, help me get back together." His words were slurred as he spit out a couple of teeth.

I examined Specimen 1. His wounds from where she had placed implants were infected; his chest was swollen, puffy with rigor mortis. His hands were green as they died.

I had to help my Specimen 1, but I wasn't certain it was possible.

"Don't worry, we'll have you back together in no time," I promised him.

But I didn't know how I was going to do that.


I went into my laboratory and stared at the replicas of his body, but I knew false body parts wouldn't fix what was happening to him. He was already dead and Specimen 5 hadn't reanimated him properly. Even getting a different body wouldn't help since the implants were gone and I couldn't put his essence into a new one.

*Journal*

He's back at work on the computer and seems delighted to be writing again. He was still bandaged from the waist up, yet there were no bandages from his elbows down. His head was unbandaged too. It was too hard for him to type all tightly bound up.

I stood in his doorway and watched his puffy fingers click away at the keyboard. He looked over at me and grinned, his beautiful smile ruined by the gaps where several teeth had fallen out. He was nearly bald from clumps of hair having fallen out. Yellow-green pus oozed through the bandages.

"Mind over matter. My fingers must work." Then he typed some more, words appearing on the computer screen as beautiful and lyrical as ever.

"Miriam," he said, "I had the perfect life with you. I want to keep living it." He reached for a cigarette and tried to light it, his fingers clumsy, his black lips barely able to purse around it. He held the cigarette in his mouth as he typed a bit more. The smell of his rotting flesh offends my nostrils, but I keep pumping air freshener into his room. I continue to watch him, watch his words float up onto the screen.

Specimen 1 turned around to stand up but his hands remained on the keyboard. We both stared in horror at the hands continuing to type while he stood up. His arms didn't bleed but a massive rush of green pus spilled out. The smell was revolting and I nearly threw up.

"How?" I gasped as the hands continued to type.

Specimen 1 reached towards me, his face in anguish.

"Help me," he said. "You have to fix me."

"I can't," I told him.

I hurried away from him. His pleading followed me out of the room, but I shut and locked the door. In the monitors, I saw him raging, trying to drink from a scotch bottle with his stumps and eventually sinking to the floor in tears.

Tears ran down my own face. It was distressing to see that once beautiful body now destroyed. The brain still worked, his affection was still there for me, yet mind could not possibly win over that mess of matter.

I pored over books and notes all night, but there were no more secrets to pull from, no more connections and chemicals to cobble together my specimen.

I fell into a dark and restless sleep in the lab, my face mashed into my glasses as I snored on my journal.

*Specimen 1*

In the morning, he was dead. Really dead. His sunken bandaged body lay on the floor, flies already feasting within the spots where his flesh had split. Maggots crawled from his eyes and ears, and the stench was beyond human endurance. His hands lay on the keyboard, covered in flies.

The next phase was never to happen.

The perfection of my experiment was destroyed.

*Journal*

Experiment 698 was a failure. So close, so many times, and perhaps the final phase would have worked if Specimen 5 hadn't kidnapped me. The forced nature of affection wasn't terribly satisfying and the stress of monitoring so many specimens took a real toll on my nerves.

I've decided to settle into a life of complacency for a while, just let life happen to me.

There is always a new experiment to conduct.

There's a guest author coming to the university next month. He looks quite handsome and his books are very well written.

I think I'll make time in my schedule to attend his lecture.

# About the Author

Sèphera Girón was born in New Orleans and currently resides in Toronto. After she graduated from York University with a Bachelor of Arts Degree, she had two sons, and began her writing career. Over twenty books later, she's still loving every minute of the business. When Sèphera isn't writing, she's editing for other authors. She is also an actor, a professional tarot counsellor, and paranormal investigator. Sèphera is the Ontario Chapter President of the Horror Writers Association and a co-producer for the Great Lakes Horror Company Podcast as presented by The Library of the Damned. Sèphera has roles in *Slime City Massacre* and *Killer Rack*, both directed by Gregory Lamberson. She also performs background work on various television shows and movies in Toronto.

http://sepheragiron.ca

http://tarotpaths.blogspot.ca

http://sephwriter666.blogspot.ca

http://www.twitter.com/sephera

Get the behind the scenes scoop by following Sèphera on Patreon!

Special thanks goes to number one patron: **Jehovah Findler**

Magnificent thanks goes to other loyal patrons:

**Somer Canon**

**Linda D. Addison**

**Brian Keene**

**Jack of Spades**

http://www.patreon.com/sephera

Visit Sèphera's YouTube channel for horoscopes, book readings, and more!

http://www.youtube.com/sephera

Made in the USA
Middletown, DE
21 September 2021